# DANG

A Humorous Mystery

_____

## R.D. SMITH

Bright Aurora Media

ISBN: 978-1-7320606-0-9

*To my wife, Erika, for everything.*
*To my dad, Dad, for the help and support.*

## Chapter One

Willem woke up and slipped a pinch of Skoal in before getting out of bed. He could see the sunlight shining through the tiny bedroom window of his single-wide trailer. Just after sunrise usually was the best time for him to collect. That was four hours ago. Another thirty minutes passed before he was up and moving. He squeezed into the bathroom, rubbed his stubbly head and splashed warm water on his face. He peeked back at his wife, Cindy, still asleep on the waterbed, then stumbled into the kitchen. He pushed his broken coffee maker aside and boiled water for a cup of instant. The stretched-out neck of his Dale Earnhardt t-shirt made it easy to pull over his head while sipping his coffee. His jeans, which he grabbed from the laundry pile beside the couch, fit a little tight around the gut he'd put on in the past year as he bent over to tie his work boots. He put on his Bassmaster cap, bent the brim and headed out the door.

Murven was already waiting by Willem's pieced-together Ford F-150. Neither spoke right away. Willem figured Murven was still upset at him for calling Luna a "high-end road whore" the night before. That used to be true, but Murven and Luna, his on-again, off-again wife, had both finally gotten over each other's pasts. They didn't need Willem "diggin' up those bones." Murven hopped in the truck as Willem lifted the tarp over the bed, grabbed a tire tool and tightened the left rear wheel so the damn thing wouldn't fall off again. Willem took one last look at his load, tied down the tarp and jumped in the driver's seat. The truck sputtered to a start and Willem jerked it into gear. The old Ford rattled out of the trailer park, and they rode in silence through the county backroads as the pickup struggled its way through the rolling hills. Willem still wasn't sure if Murven was upset about his comment or if he even remembered. Oh, well.

"You not workin' today?" Willem said.

"Nah," Murven said, "job got shut down. Not sure if it's gonna restart or not."

Murven, like most of the trailer park tenants, worked on and off. Construction jobs had been hard to get since the recession. Even if you could get one, it didn't last. Murven didn't care, though. He knew how to get by. He decided to start helping Willem on his free days. Luna was pregnant again, and her moods were swinging like a tire swing on a short rope. Murven planned to stay out of the house as much as possible until the baby was born, and probably afterwards, too. He'd been curious about Willem and his business, anyhow.

For the last year, Willem had been running what he called a biofuel/fertilizer supply company. He saw a TV show about the many uses of cow manure and horse manure. He knew where to find plenty of cow shit and horse shit, so he figured it just made sense for him to collect it and sell it. So far, he hadn't made any sales. So far, he hadn't had any prospects either. So far, all he had was a giant pile of shit he added to every day. Willem was dedicated, though, and he spent most days collecting. He had mixed feelings about Murven tagging along. Murven didn't like work much and mostly worked hard at getting out of it.

Willem and Murven cruised down a long stretch of highway where they used to drag race their hot rods as teenagers. Willem pulled off the road and drove into a "Class 1" field. Willem had created a classification system for his collecting grounds. He only had two categories. "Class 1" meant good for collecting, and "Class 2" meant bad for collecting. Willem liked to keep things simple.

Murven got out first and grabbed a bucket and a shovel. Willem did the same and they headed off in search of as much cow crap and horse crap as they could find. They both filled their buckets and headed back to the truck.

"So this is collectin'?" Murven asked.

"Yep."

"This is what you do every day?"

"Yep."

"You ever find anything besides shit?"

"Yep. Been findin' a lot of teeth," Willem said.

"Tell Peggy," Murven said. "She lost a set a week or so ago."

"Nah, I mean lots of different teeth. Sometimes the whole tooth, with roots and all."

"You think they're human teeth?" Murven asked.

Willem shrugged his shoulders, spit and walked away. He worried that finding a human tooth would bring unwanted attention to him, his collecting grounds and his new business. He knew what the police did to crime scenes and the people involved. He didn't need any of that. Just as soon as he thought about all the trouble it would bring, Murven said, "Let's call the law!"

"What the hell for?"

"This could be the break you're looking for," Murven said. "You're an entre-manure. Think of the free publicity. You could be all over the news!"

That's the last thing Willem wanted. He'd been on the news before. It wasn't worth it. He put his head down and went back to collecting.

He couldn't help thinking about the teeth he'd collected. He'd found about fifty teeth, all together. He had no idea who they belonged to or how many different people. They turned up in different places, all within about five miles from the trailer park. At first he didn't think much of it. Plenty of people he knew were missing teeth. But after about thirty or so, it started to seem weird.

"Come on!" Willem hollered, after he emptied his second bucket into the truck. "I gotta run see Poot!"

Pete Barber, or Poot, as people called him behind his back, owned the trailer park and the majority of the town. He was the landlord, bank, bail bondsman and guidance counselor for most of the trailer park tenants. He was a good guy. People trusted him. He was just gassy as hell. Willem was two months behind on his rent. He hoped Poot was in a forgiving mood.

The town was quiet as they coasted down the

main street. The few people they did see kept to themselves and went about their business. Willem parked behind the real estate office. Poot asked him not to park in the front because the odor was running people off. Anyone who'd ever spent five minutes in Poot's office would wonder why the hell that even mattered.

Willem jumped out of the truck and said, "I'll be right back."

"A'ight."

"Make sure the BFF is covered, will ya?"

"BFF?" asked Murven.

"Bio fuel slash fertilizer. B. F. F."

"That ain't what BFF means," Murven hollered.

"It is to me," Willem said, as he disappeared behind the door.

Murven adjusted the camouflage cap on his curly brown hair and took off the plaid flannel shirt he had on over his dirty white t-shirt. He tossed his shirt in the truck and picked up a stick to poke through the BFF. He figured he'd see if he could find any teeth or anything else interesting.

Willem walked into the real estate office. He paused to look at the new buck Poot had mounted on the wall. He knew Poot didn't hunt, so Willem figured he took it as somebody's rent payment. Poot did what he could to help people. Willem liked that about him. He nodded at Sandy, Poot's assistant and daughter-in-law, and eased into Poot's office.

"How you, Pete?"

"'Bout 60-40. You?"

"Same ole."

"How's business? You sell anything yet?"

"Not yet, but it'll happen."

Willem liked the way Poot showed interest without being judgmental. Most people told Willem he was a dumbass. Not Poot.

"Well, we need to work something out, Willem. You're two months behind on rent. When do you think you can pay?"

"Uh, not sure, Pete. What're my options?"

"I guess the best option is for you to sell some of the bio fuel slash fertilizer you been stockpilin' and pay me some money. But I'm not sure what the chances are for that. How much of that stuff you got now, anyway?"

"I don't know really. Good bit."

"You still keepin' it in the barn out there on your family's property?"

"Yep."

"You still not ready to sell that land? I'll buy it from ya."

"I can't sell it on my own. I gotta get my brothers to agree. That ain't happenin' anytime soon."

"A'ight, then. How 'bout doin' some work for me to cover the rent?"

"Whatchya got in mind?"

"I don't know yet. Lemme get back to ya."

"Sounds good, Pete. 'Preciate it. Lemme know if you come across anybody that needs any bio fuel slash fertilizer."

"Yep. See ya later, Willem."

"See ya, Pete."

Willem walked out of Poot's office happy that the conversation didn't take any longer than it had. He wasn't sure which reeked worse, his BFF or Poot's office. He gave Sandy another nod and headed out the door.

"Willem! Willem!" Murven hollered. "You ain't gonna believe what I found!"

"Ah, shit," Willem said. "I'm starting to feel like the damn tooth fairy."

"Oh hell no! It ain't no tooth, man! It's better than that!"

Willem couldn't imagine what he meant by "better." He wasn't sure he even wanted to know.

"I was pokin' through the BFF and I found this!" Murven said, as he tossed something at Willem.

Willem jumped out of the way. He looked down at the ground and a finger bounced to a stop at his feet.

"Geez, man! What the hell? Why you throwin' that thang at me? Which part of the BFF you find that in, Murven?"

"The pile over behind your side. We collected that today. I was with ya. We have to call the law now!" Murven said. He didn't have the same hang-ups as Willem about being a part of a police investigation.

Willem kicked the finger into the gutter and hopped in his truck. He shot Murven an annoyed glance. Without saying a word, Murven got in the truck and they headed off to the stockpile. Neither spoke at first. Willem tried to think his way out of all this while Murven worked on what to say and which hat to wear when the local news interviewed him. Murven, not sure whether or not he waited long enough, finally broke the silence. "How y'all getting by these days anyways?" he said.

"Cindy's workin' some. Credit card, mostly."

"Damn. Wish I had one of those," Murven said.

"A wife that worked?"

"Nah. Credit card."

Willem and Murven slipped back into their own thoughts. Willem turned onto a gravel road and drove for about half a mile. Murven examined the remains of the burned-down old farmhouse as they drove by. He knew better than to ask Willem about the house, the land and his relationship with his four brothers. The brothers were caught in a heated property battle. Each refused to sell his share of the land just to spite the others. If the brothers knew Willem was stockpiling BFF in the old barn, shit would hit the fan. Fortunately for Willem, his brothers lived out of state and none of them had stepped foot on the property since their parents had died in the house fire a year and a half ago.

Willem backed his truck into the barn and stopped at the base of the BFF pile. Murven leaned out of the passenger side window to get a good look at the stockpile. The BFF pile stood about twice as high as the truck and the base covered the entire back end of the barn.

"So this is a year's worth of collectin', huh?" Murven asked, as he jumped out of the truck and approached the stockpile.

"You're probably better off not steppin' in it, too," Willem said while he tightened the left rear wheel.

"How the hell can you stand this stench, man?"

"You get used to it. Get a shovel, Murven, and start unloading the truck."

Murven grabbed a shovel and worked his way around to the back side of the pile. Willem was used to the way Murven had trouble getting to work right away and ignored him for the most part. As Willem shoveled out the truck, Murven searched through the BFF with his shovel.

"Oh, shit!" Murven hollered. "Oh, hell, yeah!"

"What is it, man?

"Oh, hell, yeah! We're gonna be on the news for sure, now!"

"Murven! What the hell!"

"Just come back here, man!"

Willem jumped down from the truck bed and hurried around the BFF. He saw Murven poking at something in the shit pile with his shovel. Once Willem made his way all the way around, he could finally see what had Murven so excited.

"We're gonna be on the news!" Murven said, as Willem leaned in towards the BFF.

Willem couldn't believe what he was seeing. A limp human arm, pasty under the layer of shit, in his biofuel/fertilizer. Willem stepped back, bent the brim of his cap, and spit. He looked up at Murven, who was grinning and putting a pinch of Skoal in at the same time, and said, "Dang."

## Chapter Two

Sheriff Calvin "Happy" Maddocks and Deputy Calvin Maddocks, Jr.—CJ, for short—rolled to a stop in front of Willem's truck. Sheriff Happy stretched his long left leg out of the car and placed his size-14 foot on the ground as he stepped out of his vehicle. Deputy CJ bounced in the passenger seat as the car sprang back to its usual height. Law enforcement was the Maddocks' family business. Sheriff Happy replaced his father, Sheriff Pappy, who replaced his father, Sheriff Poppy, as the head of county law enforcement. Deputy CJ was next in line, but he failed to embrace the opportunity with the same enthusiasm as his father, grandfather and great-grandfather had. According to most county residents, he failed to do many things the same way as his elders.

Willem and Murven sat on the corral fence beside the barn and watched as Sheriff Happy strutted towards them while Deputy CJ, who stood a good foot shorter and was much less imposing than his father, walked closely behind, writing in his notebook. Sheriff Happy pointed back at his car and said, "Get in the back seat, boys," as he walked past them and moseyed into the barn. Deputy CJ looked up from his notebook long enough to see what was going on and followed his daddy through the barn door.

Willem and Murven didn't move. After a few minutes, Deputy CJ trotted out of the barn, his blond hair bouncing under his regulation cowboy hat, and said, "Deddy says you two better git your asses in that car right now."

Willem and Murven both mumbled, "A'ight," and jumped off the fence. Deputy CJ put his pen in the spiral binding of his notebook and escorted them to the squad car. Murven and Willem got into the back seat and Deputy CJ slammed the door shut. Murven fidgeted with the seat belt and door handle. He opened and closed the driver's side rear door quickly, just to see if he could.

Willem watched Deputy CJ, who sat in front of him in the passenger seat with his legs out the door. The deputy looked off into space, wrote something in his notebook, and gazed into space again.

"What're you doin'?" Willem asked.

"Tryin' to figure out how to get vampires into the story," Deputy CJ said.

"Say what?" Willem and Murven said in unison.

"Vampires. You gotta have vampires in your story these days if ya wanna git published."

"What the hell, man? I thought they took you off the crime beat at the paper," Willem said.

"Yeah," Murven said, "nobody believed half the shit you wrote."

"The vampires are for the book I'm gonna write about this, y'all. Damn. Not the newspaper."

"You're writin' books now?" Willem said.

"Yep. Crime novels. It's my callin', and this here's gonna be my inspiration," said the deputy.

"Hell, no!" Willem shouted.

"Make me look good!" said Murven.

"Hell, yeah!" the deputy said, as he gave Murven a high-five through the steel mesh partition.

Before Willem could say anything, the door opened and the car sank from the weight of the sheriff's arm resting on the roof. Sheriff Happy leaned into the car and said, "What the hell are you up to, Willem?"

"Not a damn thang, Sheriff Happy, I swear."

"You call the news yet, Sheriff?" Murven said, as he leaned in front of Willem.

"Murven, shut your mouth, son. If you ask me that again, I'm gonna tell everybody you had nothin' to do with any of this."

Sheriff Happy wrapped his enormous hand around Willem's right arm and yanked him out of the car. The sheriff walked Willem, who was on his tiptoes, to the back of the squad car and stood him against the trunk. Willem, never one to back down, locked eyes with Sheriff Happy. The sheriff took off his hat and scratched his shiny, bald head.

"You better tell me sumpin', boy," he said to Willem.

"I ain't got nuttin' to say, Sheriff."

"This don't look good, Willem. First a suspicious fire out here that killed your folks. Now a dead body."

"I didn't have nothin' to do with that fire, Sheriff. My name was cleared."

"Barely."

"Barely nothin'. You know it was all bullshit. It was trial by media. Most of it was bullshit your own son was writin'. You better watch him, too. He's about to do it again."

"I don't know what's goin' on here, son," the sheriff said, as he crossed his arms and looked down at Willem, "I think you might be losin' it."

"Bullshit."

"Normal people don't keep shit in a barn like this, boy."

"It's bio fuel slash fertilizer. That's a real thang. Look it up. Besides, why the hell would I call you if it was me?"

"Because you ain't right in the head," Sheriff Happy said, as he snatched Willem's arm, dragged him around the car and shoved him in the back seat.

"Git the tape," he said to Deputy CJ.

The deputy pounced out of the car like a scolded puppy. He grabbed the crime scene tape from the trunk and scuttled into the barn. Sheriff Happy made a quick call on his phone. The rear hubs of the squad car swallowed the tires as the sheriff leaned against the trunk in wait.

Murven packed his Skoal and offered a pinch to Willem. Willem waved the can away without taking his eyes off the road that lead down to the barn.

"What's happenin'?" Murven asked.

"He thinks it's me."

"Again?"

"Yep."

Willem and Murven watched as Deputy CJ ran in and out of the barn while Sheriff Happy held his position and kept his eyes fixed on the road. "Shit," Willem said, when a brand new gray Cadillac turned off the highway and crawled past the burned-down farmhouse to the barn. The Cadillac stopped a few feet from Sheriff Happy.

Chief County Commissioner Terrence Bristol took off his Ray-Bans and placed them in the passenger seat, on top of his real estate brochures for foreclosed beach houses in Florida. He admired himself in the rearview mirror, slicked back his naturally blond hair and attempted to rub the wrinkles off his unnaturally orange-brown forehead. He opened the door and examined the ground before stepping out in his Italian leather dress shoes. Without acknowledging the sheriff, who stood a few feet away, he closed the door and made a few last minute adjustments to his navy blue suit and tie, using his reflection in the driver's-side window.

"What's this jackass doin' here?" Murven said.

"Couldn't tell ya," Willem replied. Before Murven could say anything, Willem put his finger to his lips and leaned his head out the open door.

"What's so important you couldn't tell me over the phone?" the commissioner said. "I had to cancel a tannin' appointment to get out here."

The sheriff looked over his shoulder and into the back seat before he spoke. Willem shifted his weight and recoiled his head. Deputy CJ made his way towards the car, fidgeting with his phone while he walked, and stood behind his daddy. The commissioner paced as the sheriff reported the details.

"Goddammit!"

The commissioner cussed so loud that Willem and Murven jumped in their seats. Commissioner Bristol composed himself before poking his head into the car without touching the door or the roof. He hated getting his hands dirty.

"You're bound and determined to ruin this county, aren't ya, Willem?" the commissioner said. "First the fire, and now this. It's like you want people to stay away. I'm workin' my ass off to rejuvenate this area and you're on a killin' spree."

Willem started to speak, but Murven lurched in front of him and said, "Y'all call the news yet?" Sheriff Happy reached over the commissioner and pounded the roof of the car. The commissioner almost jumped into Willem's lap, but stopped himself. Murven laughed and spit into his dip bottle.

"Shut the hell up, Murven," the commissioner said, still jittery from the sheriff's car pounding. "Nobody's callin' the news until we figure out what the hell Willem's been up to out here."

"Well, actually..." Deputy CJ said, holding his cell phone in the air and twisting it with his wrist.

"Dammit, Junior!" Sheriff Happy hollered, as he

snatched the phone. "Git your ass back in that barn and keep workin'!"

"Shit!" Commissioner Bristol said. "We better do somethin' before the news gits here, Happy." He left the door open and walked to the back of the car with the sheriff.

Willem leaned back in the seat, took a deep breath, and then put his head between his knees again. "I didn't do this shit, Murven," he said.

"I know," Murven said, as he put his hand on Willem's back.

Willem sat up and listened to the sheriff and commissioner while Murven watched the road.

"You think he's capable of this?" the commissioner said, brushing off his suit.

"I always thought he started that fire. We just couldn't prove it. I think that boy really is losin' it, Terry."

"That's what I'm thinking, too."

"Now another dead body out here. Right in the middle of Willem's shit fuel or whatever he calls it."

"He definitely looks like the prime suspect at this point."

Willem gritted his teeth and dropped his head between his legs again. Murven took his eyes off the road long enough to see Willem wipe the sweat from his face. Willem tilted his head up towards Murven and said, "They ain't never gonna believe it's not me." Murven, not knowing what to say, shook his head and looked back towards the road.

"Whadd'ya wanna do, Happy?"

"Take'm in, I reckon."

"What about Murven?"

Murven yanked the door handle and kicked the door open. "What about Murven?!" he said, as he pulled himself out of the car. "I hadn't done shit, Sheriff!"

"Murven, stay where you are, son," the sheriff said.

Murven's jaw dropped. He knew better than to push the sheriff too hard, and he ducked his head in the door to look at Willem, who still had his head between his knees. Murven thrust himself back when he heard Deputy CJ holler, "Deddy! Deddy! I found another one!"

The sheriff and the commissioner spun around.

"Goddammit! How many bodies you got in there, Willem?" the commissioner shouted, as he slapped the trunk of the car.

Willem sprang out of the car. He stood, shaking his head, shifting his eyes from the sheriff to the commissioner, unable to speak. Murven spit out his dip, moved away from the squad car and packed his can of Skoal for a fresh pinch. Deputy CJ, dirty and out of breath, ran up to his daddy.

"Whadd'ya want me to do, Deddy?"

"Cuff 'em."

Willem didn't resist. He turned and put his arms behind his back. Deputy CJ fumbled to get his cuffs out of the case.

"You, too, Murven," the sheriff said, as he trapped Murven between himself and the car.

"Me?!" Murven hollered. "I didn't do shit! Tell 'em, Willem! This is my first day on the job."

"He's talkin' about workin'," the commissioner said. "Now I know he's lyin.'"

"Shut up and put your hands on your head, boy," the sheriff said.

Murven put his dip in his pocket and followed the sheriff's orders. As a trouble-making teenager, he had learned not to mouth off to the sheriff. Sheriff Happy slapped the cuffs on Murven and shoved him towards the car. Deputy CJ, lacking his daddy's grace with a set of handcuffs, pinched Willem's skin with the cuffs as he clasped them shut.

Willem didn't flinch. He just stared over the hood of the car at Murven, clenched his jaw, and said, "Dang."

## Chapter Three

The sheriff's office sat in the center of town next to the county courthouse. The small brick building had one jail cell and one private room that served as Sheriff Happy's office and interrogation room. Willem, cuffs removed, slouched in a squeaky desk chair in the office, waiting for the sheriff. Murven sprawled on the bed in the cell, spitting in his dip bottle—the sheriff let him have it to keep him quiet— as he watched Deputy CJ fill out reports. The sheriff had dropped Willem and Murven off at the office and headed back to process the crime scene with two other deputies. That was three hours ago.

Just after sunset, the sheriff and the commissioner stormed in, and without saying a word, marched straight to the sheriff's office. Murven bounced upright on the bed, and Deputy CJ rocked himself to his feet and followed them.

Sheriff Happy slammed the door in the deputy's face.

"Willem," he said, "you better tell me what's goin' on here, son. This really don't look good for ya."

"We found the body and called ya, Sheriff Happy. That's all I know."

The commissioner stood in the corner and slicked back his hair, content to let the sheriff conduct the interrogation for the time being. The sheriff stood in front of Willem and towered over him as he stared down.

"We found four bodies in your pile of shit, boy," said the sheriff. "The one y'all reported and three more."

Willem's heart sank and he felt sick. He leaned back in the chair and looked up at the sheriff.

"Say that again," he said.

"We found four bodies in the barn. On top of that, we searched your truck and found a bunch of teeth and some fingers in all that shit you got back there."

"I've been findin' teeth for a while now. I dunno where they're comin' from. I sure as hell don't know shit about the fingers."

"Why didn't you say sumpin'?" the commissioner asked, inching out of the corner, sensing Willem's agitation.

"Why would I?" Willem said, as he wrenched his neck back. "They were just teeth. There's people without teeth all over the damn place. And today was the first day I saw a finger."

The sheriff moved behind his desk and took a seat. "The thing is, Willem," he said, "ever since the fire, I ain't been so sure about you."

"What?" Willem said. He could see where this was heading.

"Me neither," the commissioner said from behind Willem.

Willem couldn't speak. He felt his chest pounding and the sweat running down his face. His gut told him they were going to pin this on him. Just like they tried to do with the fire and his parents' death.

"We still don't know who started that fire out at your parents' place," said the sheriff, confirming Willem's gut feeling. "You were cleared, but only because there was no hard evidence. You had motive and plenty of damn opportunity."

"Why the hell would I kill my parents?" Willem shouted. "Why?"

"You needed money and you knew they had that

insurance policy," the sheriff said, as he stood up. "And watch that tone."

"I done told you I never knew nothin' about that insurance policy. My brothers did, though. Did you ask them about the fire?"

"Willem," the commissioner said, "you kept your landscapin' equipment in the barn. After the fire, they searched the barn and all your gas cans were missin'. The fire marshal confirmed the fire was started with gas."

"I put the gas cans in my truck. I was gonna fill 'em. I told you that," Willem said through his teeth.

"Then why weren't they in your truck after the fire, boy?" the sheriff said.

"I told you that, too. They were stolen."

"Conveniently," Commissioner Bristol said. "The only thing you didn't do was read that insurance policy before you started that fire. Then you would'a known that the insurance company doesn't pay out for arson."

Willem squeezed his hands into fists and bounced his legs so hard his heels hurt. He'd been through this conversation a hundred times after the fire with every authority in the county and the state. There was no point in going there again. They didn't believe him then and they sure as hell wouldn't believe him now. Not after finding four bodies in his BFF.

"What proof do you have I killed those four people, Sheriff?" he asked.

"They're buried in your shit pile, for one," the sheriff said, "and we found body parts all over your truck. I'd say that's a pretty good start. I'm sure we'll find more evidence that points to you."

Willem kept his mouth shut. He spoke too much after the fire and gave the authorities too much ammunition to use against him. He wasn't going to make that mistake again. Sheriff Happy and the commissioner waited for Willem to lash out and defend himself, but the anger they saw a year and a half ago never appeared this time around.

"Junior!" the sheriff hollered through the closed door. Deputy CJ, who'd been standing outside eavesdropping, waited a few seconds and opened the door.

"Take him to the cell, Deputy," the sheriff ordered.

Deputy CJ waved Willem towards the cell, locked him in, and returned to the office. Willem and Murven watched the three officials through the open office door as they discussed what to do next. Murven tilted his head as he sized up the three men.

"You ever notice how Deputy CJ looks a lot like

Commissioner Bristol?" Murven whispered. Deputy CJ looked back at them and closed the door.

"What'd they tell ya?" Murven asked.

"They think it's me, pretty much. They've decided. Now they just gotta prove it."

"What about me?"

"I don't know."

"You told 'em I'm not involved in this mess, didn't ya?"

"I told 'em you had nothin' to do with it. I told 'em I didn't either. It don't matter what I say, Murven. They're not listenin' to me."

"What the hell, man? They gonna let me go or what?" Murven got up and grabbed the bars. "Hey!" he hollered. "Y'all can't keep me in here!"

Deputy CJ walked out of the office and closed the door. "Murven, Deddy says you better shut your mouth or he's gonna shut it for ya."

"What's goin' on, CJ?" Murven asked.

The deputy didn't say a word. He sat down at his desk and wrote in his notebook. Murven cussed to himself and flopped down on the bed. Willem stood up and rested his head against the bars as he watched the deputy write. Willem could see the crafty wheels turning in the deputy's head as he looked up at the jail cell and then back at the office. Deputy CJ pushed his chair back, tiptoed toward the office and put his ear to the door. He listened for a couple minutes, then tiptoed over to Willem and Murven and said in a low voice, "We have an opportunity here for a symbiotic relationship, boys."

Willem shook his head and went to the back of the cell. Murven squinted his eyes for a second and said, "What?"

"He means we can help each other, Murven."

"That's right," the deputy said. "You're goin' down for this, Willem, I can guarantee that. Unless you can prove you're innocent."

"What about me?" Murven asked, "I didn't do shit."

"That's not what Deddy and the commissioner think," Deputy CJ said, looking over his shoulder at the office.

"He's bullshittin', Murven," Willem said.

"A'ight," the deputy said, backing away. "Take your chances then. I don't give a shit. But we do have an opportunity here, y'all."

"What opportunity?" Murven asked.

"I'm not gettin' involved with this dumbass, Murven."

"Just hear me out," the deputy said, as he moved in close to the cell. Murven leaned in, almost face to face with the deputy, and Willem took a few steps closer.

"This is what I'm proposin'," the deputy said. "I'll let y'all haul ass on outta here if y'all agree to keep feedin' me tidbits to pepper my story with while you're on the run."

"Hell, no!" Willem said. "If I run, it makes me look even more guilty."

"If you don't run, your ass is goin' to prison for life," the deputy said, as he glanced back at the office door again. "The only way for you to prove you're innocent is to get out and find some proof yourself. Nobody else is gonna do it for ya."

Willem believed the deputy. His chances of beating this in court didn't look good. Sheriff Happy and Commissioner Bristol had already decided he was guilty.

"I think Willem should run, too," Murven said, still face to face with the deputy, "but why should I run? I didn't do jack shit."

"Murven," the deputy said, shaking his head, "you're guilty by association. Deddy and the commissioner think you're in on it. That's what they're talking about right now."

"Bullshit," Willem said, as Murven turned his head to try and hear the sheriff and the commissioner in the office. Deputy CJ put his hands in the air and turned back towards his desk.

Willem, realizing he didn't have much choice if

he wanted to stay out of prison, said, "What's the deal, CJ? Why do you wanna help us?"

"Symbiotic," Deputy CJ said, turning around and tapping his temple. "Y'all feed me tidbits for my story. I'll help you stay ahead of the law. It's that simple. Symbiotic."

"Last time you wrote shit about me, I damn near went to prison," Willem said. "I ain't so sure about givin' you shit for your damn book, CJ."

"The tidbits ain't for my book. I'm gonna write the newspaper story first," the deputy whispered. "I'll write the truth, which'll come from your tidbits, and that'll give me the exposure I need to transition the true story into a fiction book with vampires or zombies or sumpin' like that in it."

Willem looked at Murven, who had started to sweat. "Are they really blamin' Murven, too?" he asked. The deputy nodded. Willem could see the deputy was up to something, but at the same time he knew the only way to clear his name was to break out and prove his own innocence. He looked straight into the deputy's eyes and said, "I swear, if you screw me over you're goin' down with me, CJ."

The deputy raised his right hand and said, "Symbiotic."

"You in or out, Murven?" Willem asked.

"I'm in," Murven said, "but if you don't keep up your end, CJ, I'm comin' for ya."

The deputy put his hand through the bars and shook hands with Willem and Murven. He reached back to his desk, took his keys, listened for a moment, and then unlocked the cell. Willem and Murven kept one eye on the office while they made their way to the front door. Murven yanked the door open and bolted out. Willem took one last look at Deputy CJ, slinked out the door and whispered, "Dang."

## Chapter Four

Cindy sat glued to the couch, biting her nails, taking in every second of the breaking news on TV. The reports made her cringe. Four bodies discovered in Willem's biofuel/fertilizer. Unbelievable. Suspects Willem and Murven on the run. Countywide manhunt under way. Impossible. After eight years of marriage, Cindy knew her man Willem better than anyone. No way he could have committed four murders.

With her husband in the center ring of a media circus again, Cindy had to brace herself for the ruthless swarm of invasive coverage by TV reporters, newspaper snoops, Internet bloggers and every other wannabe newscaster, just like after the fire that killed Willem's parents. Everyone blamed him back then. The trailer park gossip patrol, spearheaded by Peggy, the self-professed trailer park news correspondent and public relations representative, made sure to expose Willem and Cindy's money problems, substantiating Willem's alleged motive for arson. Cindy turned off the TV and prepared for Peggy's inevitable knock.

As she changed from gray sweats into jeans and a clean t-shirt and brushed her long, black hair, she heard a shout.

"Cindy! Cindy! Open the damn door! You watchin' the news? Willem tried to kill Murven! Open the damn door!"

"Shit," Cindy said to herself. She peeked out the window to see who was banging on the door and accidentally made eye contact with Luna, who was peering in at the same time. She yanked the door open and demanded, "Git in here, Luna, before somebody hears you."

Luna had a deep, raspy smoker's voice that carried like a foghorn.

"Willem tried to kill my husband!" Luna shouted, as she stepped inside, pulling up her bright pink jeggings and tugging down on her matching halter-top, creating a bright pink border around her baby bump.

"Where did you hear that?" Cindy said, looking around before slamming the door shut.

"It's all over the news!" Cindy tried to speak, but Luna kept going. "Murven went collectin' with Willem today. Or at least that's what Willem said they was gonna do. Turns out Willem was gonna kill Murven and bury him in that shit pile o' his."

"What news are you watching, Luna? I didn't hear anything about Willem tryin' to kill Murven. From what I heard, it sounds like they're on the run together." Luna had a reputation in the trailer park for distorting the news.

"Whatever, the point is your husband got my husband in a whole heap'a trouble."

Luna plopped down on the recliner next to the couch and leaned over to turn on the TV. Cindy caught a glimpse of Luna's peek-a-boo tattoo that used to be either a beaver or a rabbit, but five pregnancies and too much fast food had turned it into what appeared to be a roadkill tramp stamp. Luna listened intently for a minute, then, with surprising agility for a pregnant woman, sprang to her feet and said, "The reporter just said they was packing up and headed this way. I gotta run put the 'for sale' sign on Murven's truck. Maybe somebody will see it on the news and wanna buy it. I gotta check on my boys right quick, too."

"Luna! Wait! Don't go outside! Peggy is gonna see you!" Cindy shouted, but it was too late. Luna was halfway down the steps before Cindy could finish.

"Hey, Peggy," Luna said, stepping off the last step and waddling over to her trailer directly across the trailer park.

Peggy poked her head in the door without going up the steps. "Hey, there. How you doin', sugar?" she said, frothing at the mouth like a hungry dog waiting for a morsel of juicy gossip.

"I'm OK," Cindy said, as she tried to close the door. Peggy raced up the steps and jammed the door with her left hand.

"Lemme interview you right quick for my YouTube channel," she said, holding up her pocket video camera with her right hand. "This is my chance to finally git the scoop on the local news."

"No," Cindy said, pushing Peggy out the door.

"It'll just take a minute. We can sit on the couch and put my camera on your coffee table. I got a new set a' teeth, so I can do close-ups again."

Peggy was notorious for losing her teeth and for sniffing out trailer park gossip. A few years and several sets of teeth ago, Peggy wrote the trailer park newsletter, which, with all the misspellings, was virtually impossible to read for those who could read. About a year ago, she made the transition from print to video with her YouTube channel on the Internet.

With the changeover, the degree and clarity of Peggy's meddling became much more evident and led to retaliation, both physical and in various forms of media, by other trailer park residents. But that never stopped Peggy. Willem once told Cindy he thought Peggy's YouTube channel would most likely get her killed one day, and that she was better off writing because she had a face for newsletters anyway. Cindy agreed.

"I'm sorry, Peggy, I can't do an interview right now."

"Come on now, Cindy, you know how important timin' is for this sort of thang. This is a big opportunity for me."

"This is not a good time, Peggy," Cindy said, chewing her nails.

Peggy let herself in anyway, made herself at home on the couch and fidgeted with her camera, the coffee table and her teeth. Cindy sauntered into the kitchen to put some distance between them. As she started to pour a glass of water, she heard a noise in the bedroom.

"Psssst," someone hissed.

"Peggy, let me change right quick before you put me on camera," Cindy said, as she went into her room and closed the door. "Willem?" she whispered.

Willem had installed a trapdoor in the floor of

the bedroom after the fire to evade Peggy and all the reporters. The hinges squeaked as Willem lifted the trapdoor and popped his head through.

"Willem," Cindy said, making sure the bedroom door was closed, "What the hell are you doing here? They're gonna find you. Are you OK?"

"We ain't got much time," Willem said. "I need your car keys."

"What's goin on? I've been worried sick," Cindy said.

"I really don't know. I'm innocent. Everybody thinks I'm guilty. Just like the fire."

"Why did you run? Why is Murven with you?"

"They think he's in on it with me. I escaped to find evidence to prove I'm innocent."

"Hey, Cindy," Murven interrupted, squeezing his head through the trap door next to Willem. "You seen Luna? Has she been on the news yet?"

"She was just here," Cindy said. "The news crews are on their way. She went to put a 'for sale' sign on your truck."

"Oh, good," Murven said, "maybe somebody will see it on the news and wanna buy it."

"Do you wanna talk to Luna?" Cindy asked.

"Hell, no," Murven said. "I bet she's pissed. Don't tell her you saw us until after we're gone."

"Peggy's sittin' on the couch. Lemme get rid of

her so y'all can git outta here," Cindy said, as she rose and pressed her ear against the door. Willem and Murven lowered themselves and closed the trapdoor. Cindy waited until they were back under the trailer before opening the bedroom door.

Luna reappeared at the front door just as Cindy left the bedroom. Luna saw Peggy on the couch with the camera set up for an interview and shouted, "Y'all doin' an interview without me?"

Cindy, sensing a window of opportunity, said, "Well, of course not, Luna. I wouldn't do that to you. You know what, why don't I let Peggy interview you first? It can be a solo interview. Is that OK for you, Peggy?"

"Well, I guess so," Peggy said. "As long as I can interview you, too, before the news crews git here."

"Not a problem," Cindy said. "Luna, why don't y'all go do your interview by Murven's truck so you can get the 'for sale' sign in the shot."

"Well, hell yeah, we can do it by the truck," Luna said. "Come on, Peggy."

Cindy waited for Luna and Peggy to get to the bottom of the steps before racing back to the bedroom. She dropped down on her knees and pounded on the trapdoor. Willem squeezed his head through. "Is the coast clear?" he asked.

"As clear as it's gonna be. But how are you gonna

git to my car without being seen? It's parked right in front of the trailer."

"Shit," Willem said, "I hadn't thought about that. Maybe you can go somewhere and pick us up down the road."

"I don't know. Peggy's watchin' me pretty close."

"Cindy! Cindy!" Peggy shouted from outside. "The news crews are comin' down the road! I see the headlights!"

Willem dropped back down and closed the trap-door. Cindy slammed the bedroom door shut and rushed out the front door.

"We gotta do the interview quick," Peggy said, grabbing Cindy's arm and pulling her back into the trailer. "I gotta git it posted on YouTube."

"We don't have time," Cindy said, resisting Peggy's tugging. "Why don't you post the interview with Luna. You can still get the scoop with that, can't ya?"

"I reckon. But you owe me sumpin' big now," Peggy said, as she scurried back to her trailer to upload the video. Cindy was sure owing Peggy "sumpin' big" would come back to bite her in the ass eventually.

Luna, who had gone into her trailer after her interview, stepped outside with her four boys and walked over next to Cindy. "I wonder where the hell Willem and Murven are right now," Luna said.

"Wish I knew," Cindy said, looking over her shoulder at her own trailer.

Cindy, Luna and the four boys watched as the cars sped toward the trailer park. When the vehicles got close enough to see them through the darkness, they discovered it wasn't news crews after all. Cindy chewed her nails, looked back at the trailer again and said, "Dang."

## Chapter Five

Sheriff Happy turned into the Sunny Bluff Trailer Park and coasted to a smooth stop in front of Cindy, Luna and the four boys. Deputy CJ cut a corner too close in his squad car, missing the row of rusty mailboxes at the entrance by inches, and rear-ended Sheriff Happy's vehicle. The sheriff's car lurched forward, scattering the women and the four brothers. Sheriff Happy scowled at Deputy CJ in the rearview, picked up his CB and screamed, "Boy, I swear if you're writin' and drivin' again, I'm gonna rip that notebook to shreds."

"Sorry, Deddy," Deputy CJ said, hiding his face with the CB and sliding down in the seat.

Sheriff Happy's searchlight flickered off the trailers, revealing the leering eyes of residents through partially closed trailer curtains. Nobody wanted to deal with Sheriff Happy. Except Peggy. She charged outside, shooting video with one hand and adjusting her teeth with the other.

"Go back to your trailer, Peggy," Sheriff Happy warned, as he got out of his car.

"But this is breakin' news, Sheriff!"

"It's gonna have ta break later. Now git inside!"

"I'm the media, Sheriff. You're violatin' my first commandment rights."

"The Bible ain't got nothin' to do with this," the sheriff said, as he put his hand in front of the camera.

"Tsss. You're not media, Peggy," Deputy CJ snorted, pushing the camera away from his daddy. "You're trailer park tabloid trash."

"Kiss my ass, CJ," Peggy responded, turning the camera towards the deputy and then pulling it away. "Actually, I better not. I'll ruin my own credibility. Everybody knows you're full of shit, Deputy Dumbass."

The recent murders were sure to rekindle the legendary rivalry between Deputy CJ and Peggy. Before the deputy lost his position as crime reporter for the local newspaper, he and Peggy had epic name-calling and debunking battles in the newspaper and trailer park newsletter. Peggy liked to flaunt the fact that she was partially responsible for the deputy being removed from the crime beat when she "broke the story" that Deputy CJ was fabricating the facts in his reporting, something everybody already knew anyway.

"Whatever," Deputy CJ said. "I'm back at the paper now, you toothless hag. So stay outta my way."

"Knock it off," Sheriff Happy said. "Peggy, if you wanna shoot this, do it from your trailer. CJ, cut the shit." The sheriff walked over to Cindy, as the deputy shot Peggy the bird behind the sheriff's back. Peggy waved him off and positioned herself on her rickety trailer steps to shoot video.

Sheriff Happy looked at Luna and ordered, "You and the boys go to your trailer. I'll come talk to you in a minute. Cindy, tell me everything you know."

"I don't know much, Sheriff. Just what was on the news."

"Make sure you're bein' straight with me, Cindy. You always know what's goin' on with Willem. If you know sumpin', now's the time to tell me."

"I swear I don't know anything, Sheriff Happy. I didn't know anything about those bodies in Willem's BFF until I saw it on the news. It's terrible. Do you know who those people are?"

"We're workin' on it. What can ya tell me about what's goin' on with Willem and his brothers? Those Wisely boys goin' at each other again? Is Willem doin' this to get back at one of 'em? Or all of 'em?"

"Well, first off, Sheriff, Willem never killed anybody. Ever. And don't assume he's guilty unless you have evidence to prove it," Cindy said, pointing at the sheriff.

"Watch your tone, now—"

"You asked me a question, so let me speak," Cindy said, as she took a step closer to Sheriff Happy. "We hadn't heard shit from Willem's brothers since the fire. Even before the fire, we never heard much of anything. The only one of those assholes we've had any contact with is Wilbur. After Willem's arson trial, where, as you remember, he was found innocent, Wilbur went out to the barn and cleaned some stuff out. We hadn't heard shit from him, or Wilton, Willard, or Walmer since." Cindy leaned against the sheriff's squad car to catch her breath.

"The last I heard, Poot was tryin' to buy the Wisely property, but Willem and the other Wisely boys won't sell. They must be communicatin' somehow if they can all refuse Poot's offers. Some-body's talkin' to somebody."

Cindy hated the way everybody knew everybody else's business in the county. She grew up in a big city and moved to the trailer park with Willem after they got married eight years ago. She figured she'd never really get used to it. But all the gossiping,

muckraking, bad-mouthing and bullshitting gener-
ated by the county rumor mill had taught her how to
read people. She could tell Sheriff Happy knew
more than he was saying.

"They're doin' it all through lawyers," Cindy
said, as she pushed herself off the car and crossed her
arms. "From what I know, at least."

"What's Poot want with that land, anyway?"

"Hell if I know," Cindy said, which was the
truth. Willem didn't know what Poot's interest was,
either. They just assumed Poot wanted to build
another trailer park. She sensed the sheriff knew
more than he was letting on, asking loaded questions
and testing her to see what she knew. Cindy shot
back, "What do you know about it, Sheriff?"

Sheriff Happy shrugged, tilted his head to the
side and dipped his knees slightly to look straight
into Cindy's eyes. He waited for Cindy to break eye
contact and give something away, but like her
husband, she was never one to back down.

"A'ight," Sheriff Happy said. "Junior, take a look
around."

"A'ight, Deddy," Deputy CJ said. He checked
the squad cars for dents, flipped off Peggy again
when his daddy wasn't looking, dug his flashlight out
of the trunk and strolled towards the trailer. Before
using his legs to clear the way around back, he

inspected the weeds and wild grass that had grown up between Cindy and Willem's trailer and their neighbor's. He sidled into the brush and wondered how Willem ever made a living as a landscaper. After reaching a clearing behind the trailer, the deputy sucked the bloody thorn pricks on his hands and picked the hitchhikers off his pants. He surveyed the woods that stretched for a few miles beyond the trailer park, then shined his flashlight through the chicken wire Willem had installed as trailer skirting.

"Dammit!" he said. "I see you two idiots!"

Willem poked his head through the split in the chicken wire and said, "Hush, CJ! Your daddy's gonna hear you."

"Why the hell didn't y'all haul ass when you saw us comin' down the road?"

"We wanted to try and listen to what y'all said," Murven whispered, as he squeezed his head out next to Willem.

"Y'all are supposed to be on the run. This shit ain't gonna work if I keep catching your asses."

CJ jogged to the edge of the trailer to check on his daddy. Sheriff Happy and Cindy were walking towards Luna's trailer. The deputy hustled back over to Willem and Murven, who had come out from under the trailer. "Good thang Deddy brought me instead of another deputy. Y'all need to run."

"We don't know where to go, CJ," Willem said. "What do you know so far?"

"It's been half a day. We don't know shit. The forensic people are on their way."

"Then where the hell are we supposed to go? You can't tell us anything?" Willem said, as Murven drifted towards the woods.

"All we know at this point is those bodies we found don't match the descriptions of anybody reported missing. We ran the fingerprints and we didn't get any hits either."

"So what does that mean?" Murven asked from the edge of the woods in a loud whisper.

"It means those dead guys weren't missed much," Willem said.

"Yep, and Deddy said by the clothes they was wearin' they was probably homeless. He's gonna send somebody to the hobo jungle down by the tracks at the edge of the county."

"I thought you said you don't know shit. It sure as hell sounds like you do know a little sumpin', CJ," Murven said.

"So we should go down to the tracks?" Willem interrupted before a fight broke out.

"Well, yeah," Deputy CJ said, "and you better git there before some deputy does. Once the law starts pokin' around the jungle, that place'll clear out and y'all will be shit outta luck tryin' to find somebody to talk to."

"What're we lookin' for?" Murven asked.

"Information, dipshit. See if any of those hobos know anything about people goin' missin'. And don't forget my tidbits. I need sumpin' to write about."

"A'ight," Willem and Murven said.

"Oh, hey," the deputy said, before they could take off. "Y'all think you can git your hands on a gun and pop off a few rounds? I wanna write about a gunfight."

"Hell, no!" Willem said, almost hollering.

"Never mind, then. Damn, keep it down."

Murven turned towards the woods. Willem paused and asked, "CJ, does your daddy think Cindy's in on this mess, too?"

"I don't think so. He hadn't said anything to me about it."

"What about Luna?" Murven asked over his shoulder.

"I doubt it, " CJ said. "Y'all need to git outta here. Don't forget my tidbits. Now go!"

Willem and Murven picked their way through the briar patch at the edge of the woods and Deputy CJ had pushed the chicken wire back into place when they heard someone coming around the trailer.

Willem and Murven dropped to the ground, and the deputy jumped.

"Who are you talkin' to?" Peggy said, sweeping the woods with her flashlight and camera.

"What the hell are you doin' back here?" Deputy CJ hollered. "You scared the shit out of me. More than usual, too."

"I know you were talkin' to somebody, CJ. Who was it?

"I don't have to tell you shit. Git back on the porch," the deputy said, clicking his tongue and snapping his fingers. Peggy ignored him and prowled closer to the woods, with her camera and flashlight stretched out in front of her.

Willem and Murven lay flat as possible. "I think she saw us," Murven said.

Willem watched as the light passed over their heads, spit, and whispered, "Dang."

## Chapter Six

Willem and Murven stayed low as Peggy scanned the pitch-black woods with her flashlight and camera. Murven reached for his can of Skoal, but Willem grabbed his arm and forced it to the ground.

Deputy CJ stepped in front of Peggy. The flashlight shined in his eyes as he said, "Peggy, you really can't be back here. You're interfering with an official investigation."

"I know you're up to sumpin', CJ," Peggy said, as she lowered her arms. "There's sumpin' goin' on around here and I'm gonna find out what."

"Ain't shit happenin'," the deputy said, as he nudged Peggy away from the woods. "Mind your own business."

"Bullshit. I saw Willard and Walmer Wisely

sneakin' out the back of Commissioner Bristol's office just last week."

"What?" Deputy CJ said, unable to hide his surprise.

"Oh, so you didn't know that, huh? Well, I know more than that, too. Maybe we should make a deal?"

"I ain't makin' no deals with you. Now git on back to your trailer steps."

Deputy CJ shooed Peggy away. She flipped her camera closed, listened for signs of movement in the woods, then walked back around the trailer and ambled through the weeds. The deputy looked back towards the spot where he last saw Willem and Murven, unsure whether they were still there, and then followed Peggy.

"Did you hear that?" Murven whispered, pushing himself up on his knees and reaching for his Skoal.

"Yep."

"You think Peggy knows anything?"

"Hard to say," Willem said, as he brushed off his jeans and adjusted his cap. "She's pretty damn nosey. No tellin' what she knows."

"What she said explains a lot."

"Whadd'ya mean?"

"Well, Luna told me she saw you comin' outta Commissioner Bristol's office a couple weeks ago.

She musta seen Willard or Walmer. All y'all look just alike."

"You never told me that."

"I didn't really believe her. Luna's mostly fulla shit. Guess she did see sumpin'."

"Dammit, Murven, shit like that matters right now. What else has Luna told ya?"

"Nothin' I can think of."

"Let's git outta here, then figure out how to git to the hobo jungle before the deputies."

Willem pulled Murven into the woods. They jogged along the narrow trail, unhindered by the darkness. They'd hunted and fished in these woods their whole lives. They could get from one end of the county to the other blindfolded if they had to.

"What do you think Willard and Walmer are doin' with Commissioner Bristol?" Murven said, once the trailer park was out of view. Willem shook his head and sat down on a log to catch his breath. Murven flopped down on the ground in front of Willem and asked, "You think it has anything to do with all this?"

"I couldn't tell ya. I don't know what any of my brothers are up to these days. Willard and Walmer were buddies with Commissioner Bristol growin' up. I guess they all kept in touch."

"Willard and Walmer have that truckin' company, don't they?"

"They used to. They had several companies together. But from what I heard, they had a fallin' out four or five years ago."

"What about Wilton and Wilbur?" Murven asked, counting on his fingers and trying to keep the brothers straight.

"Wilton's just an asshole that don't wanna talk to nobody. He's some kinda accountant or sumpin'. He lives alone somewhere. Wilbur owns all them pawn-shops. That's why he cleaned out the barn after the fire. He took everything he could sell. None of 'em talk to me, though."

Willem pulled his hat down over his eyes and put his elbows on his knees. Growing up the youngest of five boys, each one year apart, was tough. Willard, the oldest, and Walmer, the second son, were both star athletes and valedictorians who set the bar high for the other brothers. They both went to college on full academic scholarships and rein-vented themselves as city slickers. Wilton was the quiet middle child, content reading fantasy novels and comic books, playing video games and staying as invisible as possible. Wilbur had regular run-ins with Sheriff Happy and was convicted several times for petty theft and selling stolen property. Owning pawnshops was a natural career choice for him. Willem was the youngest, least motivated and most average of all the five brothers—the son the Wisely parents doted on the most. The other four hated him for that.

Murven opened his can of Skoal and winced at the last pinch. He decided to save it for later and said, "We need a plan. Fast!"

"Right now what we need is a ride."

"You wanna go back and try to get Cindy's car?"

"Nah, we can't go back there. We need to keep movin'."

Willem took off his hat and scratched his stubbly head. "Y'know, Poot keeps his maintenance trucks over at Shady Bluff. We're close."

"Whadd'ya sayin'? You wanna take one of Poot's trucks?"

"I don't know what else to do. We can explain to Poot later. He won't press charges."

"I don't know, " Murven said, putting a pinch of dip in out of habit, forgetting it was his last one.

"You have a better idea?"

"Nah."

"A'ight then. It's only about half a mile. Let's get movin'," Willem said, as he tightened the laces on his work boots.

Willem and Murven made it to Shady Bluff

Trailer Park in less than ten minutes. Willem scouted the area while Murven hid in the darkness of the woods and kept watch.

"How's it lookin'?" Willem said, as he knelt down next to Murven.

"A'ight, I guess. I hadn't seen anybody come out. I saw a squad car go down the road but it didn't turn in."

"How long's it gonna take you to hot-wire the truck?"

"Not long. But I don't need to hot-wire it. I know where Poot keeps the key."

"Dammit, Murven! Why don't you tell me shit like this?"

"I don't know."

Willem pushed Murven towards the truck, then crouched down, watched and waited. Murven strolled into the trailer park like he owned the place, reached up under the right front wheel hub, and felt around for the spare key. Chunks of dried mud dropped to the ground as Murven scraped them off the wheel hub and felt for the magnetic key box. Murven spit out his last pinch of Skoal and smiled when he discovered the key. He jumped in the truck, rolled down the window and hollered, "Come on!"

"Shit," Willem muttered, as he ran towards the truck. Willem checked, but no one in the trailer park came outside or even looked out a window to see what was going on.

"Ready?" Murven asked.

"Just go, dammit."

Murven cranked the truck and sped down to the road. He looked right before turning out, spotted a set of headlights, slammed the truck into reverse and shot back into the trailer park with the lights off.

"Holy shit!" Murven said. "That was close. That was Sheriff Happy."

"Yeah, I bet that first squad car you saw was Deputy CJ. We better go the back way to the tracks."

Murven inched the truck forward while shifting his head left and right. Willem looked back at the trailer park to see if anyone had seen them. Murven shrugged and Willem gave him a go-ahead nod. The rear tires slid as Murven gunned it out of the trailer park.

Murven turned off the paved road after a mile and clicked on his bright headlights. "You think this truck can handle these dirt roads?" he said.

"Maybe."

Willem looked back every few seconds while Murven drove with his right arm resting on the seat. The old Chevy pickup labored its way up and down the hills along the dirt road.

"You know what we ought to do?" Murven said.

"We ought'a shoot some video of us saying we're innocent."

Willem shook his head and stared out the passenger-side window.

"I'm serious," Murven continued. "We can tell people our side of the story. Maybe we can get some supporters. Better yet, we can get some fans!"

Willem bent the brim of his cap and cracked a smile. Murven always looked on the bright side. Even when wrongly accused of murder and on the run.

"We'll see," Willem said, wondering if Murven might be onto something. "Let's just see what we can dig up at the jungle. Then we can think about it."

"That'll work!" Murven said, slapping the dashboard. The pickup rattled down the dirt road. Murven chuckled as the truck bounced up and down the hills and the rear end swung from side to side around the curves.

"Pull over and turn off the truck," Willem said, just before hitting the paved road. "We better walk in from here." Murven drove the truck behind a tree and killed the engine.

Without speaking, Willem and Murven lurched out of the truck and took off towards the railroad tracks. The hobo jungle was about a mile down the dirt road that ran along the tracks and was well hidden from view. The encampment, situated on one of the many hills that blanketed the county, was a short-term layover point for hobos. Most never stayed for more than a day or two. The county folk steered clear of the jungle, Willem and Murven included, and the hobos kept to themselves.

Willem and Murven worked their way to the opposite side of the hill and climbed towards the top. "You wait when we reach the top," Willem said, "and I'll walk down the hill myself. If we go down together, we may run the hobos off."

"Wait," Murven whispered, putting his right hand up and crouching low to the ground. "I heard sumpin'."

Willem tapped Murven on the shoulder then inched toward the top of the hill. He maneuvered his way from tree to tree, staying hidden as he ascended. As he reached the peak, he gasped, ducked behind the nearest tree and wrenched his head back to see Murven standing face to face with someone. Willem leaned his back against the tree, unable to move for a moment, and watched the red and blue lights beam through the trees. Murven, too far down the backside of the hill to see the lights flashing from the other side, waved at Willem. Willem pushed himself off the tree and said, "Dang."

# Chapter Seven

Willem surveyed the hillside before stepping away from the tree. He squinted, but it was too dark and he was too far away to see more than the silhouette of a hat and a long coat next to Murven. He turned his head to listen to the escalating commotion on the other side of the hill as the deputies raided the hobo jungle. He looked back down the hill and paused for one last look. Murven's new buddy was too short to be Deputy CJ and too calm to be part of the raid. Willem bent the brim of his hat, spit, and sidestepped downhill towards Murven.

"It's OK," Murven said, waving Willem closer. "He's a hobo."

"What's happenin'?" Willem asked, as he slid to a stop.

"Bo here said a deputy came to the jungle and started askin' a bunch of questions. Most of the hobos ran off. The deputy called for backup to round up the hobos."

"What're they askin'?" Willem said, looking at Bo.

"They was askin' 'bout 'bos that went missin','" Bo said.

"That's all he'll say 'less we git him outta here," Murven said.

"Shit," Willem muttered. "Let's git to the truck."

Willem and Murven led Bo down the hill and along the trail. They stopped in the tree line to scope out the paved road before crossing. Willem waved his hand and Murven and Bo hunkered down in the shrubs. Willem crept to the edge of the paved road, looked and listened for squad cars, then darted across the street. Murven reached for Bo, but he was too slow. Bo took off like a sprinter shooting off the starting block. He bounded across the street, long coat flapping like a cape, and passed Willem once he saw the truck.

"Holy shit," Murven gasped, as he slammed against the truck. "Hobos can run fast as hell!"

"What do you know, Bo?" Willem said, pushing Murven to the driver's seat.

"Git me outta here. Git me sumpin' to eat. Then I'll talk."

"Shit," Willem said, "git in the truck."

Murven cranked the old Chevy and said, "Where to?"

"We need ta hide for a while," Willem said.

"We can go to my cousin Jesper's place at Windy Bluff," Murven said, as he shifted into gear.

Willem rolled down the window and aired out the cab with his hat. Bo's odor reminded him of his BFF. "Jesper." Willem groaned. Jesper was trouble, but they were desperate. "I reckon that's all we got."

Murven turned on to the dirt road and a spotlight lit up the cab. "Step out of the vehicle," the deputy said through the megaphone.

"Haul ass, Murven!" Willem shouted.

Murven stood on the gas pedal and kicked up dust as the back end of the truck swung around. The deputy flipped on his lights and sirens and chased after them.

"Git on it!" Willem hollered, rolling up the window and watching the rearview as the deputy closed in on the truck.

"I'm tryin'! This old ass pickup ain't made for this shit!" Murven tore down the dirt road, whipping around corners and grinning from ear to ear.

"Let me out!" Bo shouted.

"Tell us what you know first," Willem demanded.

"Bullshit," Bo muttered, as he braced himself with his hands on the dash.

Murven put his right arm around Bo, who was seated in the middle, clicked his teeth with a half-smile and steered with his left hand. The deputy, sliding too much around the curves, fell behind.

"I think I lost him," Murven said. "But we're in trouble when we cross over the next paved road." Willem nodded and Bo shook his head.

Murven put both hands on the wheel when the paved road came into view. Willem, watching the right side of the intersection, shouted, "Sheriff Happy comin' up fast!" Murven sped up to jump across the main road and onto the next stretch of dirt road, but the sheriff cut him off. Murven spun the wheel to the left and the pickup bounced onto the asphalt.

"I can't outrun' em, but I can outdrive 'em," Murven said, winking at Bo.

"Sheriff Happy's closin' the gap," Willem said, twisting around in his seat.

Murven raced through the next intersection and another car joined the chase. "That's CJ," Murven said, checking the mirror.

Sheriff Happy accelerated and rammed the rear of the truck. "Holy shit!" Willem shouted. "He's tryin' to run us off the road!"

The sheriff slammed into the truck again, harder, and lifted the rear wheels off the ground.

"CJ's comin' in fast!" Murven said. "He's bumper to bumper with the sheriff."

Sheriff Happy aimed the front of the vehicle like a missile and rammed the truck so hard the rear of the truck crashed down on the hood of the squad car. Deputy CJ gunned it, positioned his front bumper alongside the sheriff's rear bumper, and jerked his car hard to the right, sending both squad cars into a spin. The truck slammed down, and Willem shouted, "Hot damn! CJ just ran his daddy off the road!"

"I'm gettin' off this pavement," Murven said, as he killed the lights and steered the truck onto the grass. He drove along the edge of the tree line until he spotted a trail wide enough for the pickup. "The rear end's tore up," he said, as the truck clunked along the trail.

"Just get us to Jesper's," Willem said.

Windy Bluff Trailer Park, the sketchiest of all the trailer parks Poot owned, lay deep in the woods. Jesper, a moonshiner and wannabe pro-wrestler, ruled over the trailer park. All the tenants worked for him as bootleggers and occasionally served as wrestling practice dummies. Jesper had a big heart, small brain, and hot temper. Murven and Jesper grew up together but had grown apart over the years. Jesper's daddy, Giblet, also a moonshiner and pro-wrestler wannabe, taught the two cousins how to drive. Giblet died running shine when his car exploded during a high-speed chase.

The engine sputtered and the rear end rumbled as the pickup hobbled into the trailer park. Murven steered the truck around the stack of old mattresses that served as a wrestling ring and parked at the foot of Jesper's trailer steps.

"Stay in the truck, Bo," Murven said, as he and Willem got out of the truck. "Willem, you stand at the bottom of the steps."

Murven climbed the crooked wooden steps, looked back at Willem, then tapped lightly on the door. "Wooooo!" they heard Jesper shout from inside.

Willem took a step back and Bo slid down in his seat. Murven slapped his chest and replied, "Woooo!" Willem glanced back at the mattresses and wondered how long it would be before one them ended up on their back.

Murven dropped down a step as the door swung open. He stood face to gut with Jesper and bobbed his head, rasslin' style, at the sight of his cousin's body art. Jesper bobbed his head in return, threw his arms in the air and twisted in a victory spin. As Jesper rotated, Murven admired the way Jesper's WWE championship belt tattoo covered his beer belly, wrapped around his love handles and came together over his plumber's cleavage. The "WOOO!" tattooed on his chest sagged as Jesper lowered his arms, which were inked like monster truck coilover shocks, and pulled Murven in for a bear hug.

"What's up, Cuz?" Murven said, as his feet lifted off the steps.

"My man, Murven. Woooo! You're all over the news, son. Wooooo!" Jesper said, releasing Murven and reaching for his pistol on the wobbly table next to the door. "Who's with ya?"

"It's all good," Murven said, grabbing Jesper's hand and guiding the gun back to the table. "That's Willem."

Jesper looked at Willem and nodded. Willem nodded back as he hid behind the truck. Jesper bent his knees and looked in the pickup. He reached for his gun again and said, "Who's in the truck?"

"He's okay," Murven said, pushing the gun down. "He's got info we need. Can you help us?"

"Well, hell yeah, I can help ya. You're family. Git

in here." He pulled Murven in the trailer and hollered, "Come on, Willem. Bring that other dude with ya!"

Willem opened the truck door and said, "Let's go, Bo."

"I ain't goin' in there. That guy ain't right in the head."

"If you wanna eat, we gotta go inside. Or you can tell me what ya know now and git the hell outta here."

Bo climbed out of the truck and looked around the trailer park. His stomach growled as he considered his options.

"Reckon I'll eat."

Willem hustled up the steps and stopped at the door. Bo climbed the steps like a frightened kitten, crouching low and darting his eyes around with each step. At the last step, Willem yanked Bo up by his coat and shoved him inside.

Jesper, gun in hand, stood next to the flatscreen TV mounted to the wall with wire coat hangers. He raised the gun, pointed it at Bo, and said, "Murven says you got information. Talk."

"Wait a minute," Willem said, moving away from Bo.

"I told him to talk. Not you. Sit."

"Jesper," Murven said, twisting the top off a mason jar and taking a sip of moonshine, "He just wants sumpin' to eat, then he'll talk."

Jesper raised his pistol and fired a shot through the ceiling.

"Wooooo!" he said, bobbing his head. "I had y'all goin'! Y'all should'a seen y'all's faces. Woooo!"

Murven smiled as he picked up a can of Skoal from the kitchen counter and put in a pinch.

"A'ight, then." Willem sighed, trying to catch his breath. "You got anything to eat?"

Bo wiped the sweat off his face, dropped down to one knee and muttered, "Holy shit."

"You wanna eat?" Murven said.

"I just want outta here now," Bo said, standing up, his back sliding against the doorframe. "I'll talk."

"Git 'em sumpin', Murven," Willem said. "What were the deputies askin' 'bout, Bo?"

"They was askin' if anybody knew 'bout other 'bos disappearin'," Bo said, keeping his eyes on Jesper, who was still holding his pistol. "Nobody told 'em shit. 'Bos always go missin'."

"Anything weird goin' on at the jungle?" Willem asked.

"Not really. But the jungle 'round here's been busier than usual. Suppose to be work up this way."

"What kinda work?" Murven said, as he sat a bowl of grits on the table.

Bo headed for the bowl of grits, and without sitting down shoved a heaping spoonful in his mouth. He swallowed and said, "Not sure. Some guy been roundin' 'bos up at the jungle." He scooped another clump of grits in his mouth. "Ain't much work around. 'Bos'll do anythin' these days."

"Who's the guy?" Willem asked.

"Don't know. Never seen 'im. I heard some 'bos call 'im Willem."

"Say that name again," Willem said, grabbing Bo's wrist.

"Willem," Bo said, as he jerked his wrist away and shoveled grits in his mouth.

"Holy shit!" Murven said. "What the hell's goin' on?"

Willem's heart raced as he replayed Bo's words in his mind. All the pieces fell into place. The teeth. Four bodies in his BFF. Now a hobo dropping his name. He broke out in a sweat and cussed himself for playing straight into the setup. He walked to the door and breathed in the cool night air. He contemplated how his escape may have thrown a wrench in the perpetrator's plan and his heart began to settle. He glanced back at Murven, his best friend and alleged accomplice, and wondered if he was in this mess by chance or by design. He thought of Cindy, and even Luna a little, and then turned his thoughts to his next move. He and Murven were on the run and had no other choice now but to see this through. Willem stepped out of the trailer, bent the brim of his hat, spit, and said, "Dang."

# Chapter Eight

Willem woke up to the sound of Murven and Jesper talking in the kitchen. He sat up on the couch, rubbed his eyes and picked his cap up off the dusty floor. As he stretched his arms over his head, his eyes adjusted to the yellow sunrise lighting the trailer through the cracked windows. Murven and Jesper sat at the kitchen table, sipping on moonshine and chuckling. Bo had taken off after filling his belly. Jesper had scared him pretty good, and after learning Willem's name, his fight-or-flight instinct kicked in. Willem bent the brim of his hat, pushed himself off the couch and walked into the kitchen.

"Mornin', sunshine!" Murven shouted.

"Shit, Murven. You drunk?" Willem opened the front door and poked his head outside.

"Little bit." Murven sat up straight and smiled at

Jesper. "You better come in here. You ain't gonna believe this shit."

"Believe what?" Willem asked.

"Well, I told Jesper the whole story. Tell him what you told me, Jesper," he said, slouching back in his seat.

"I feed CJ tidbits, too," Jesper said as he took a sip of shine.

"What do you mean?" Willem looked at Murven, then out the door again.

"Me. CJ. Tidbits. You heard me."

"Tidbits about moonshinin'?" Willem nudged Murven awake.

"Sorta. Truth is, there ain't much money in moonshine these days. It's just my cover. I still use my bootleggin' skills. Just not for shine."

Willem took off his cap and rubbed his stubbly head. No telling what the hell Jesper was involved in. "What kinda tidbits are you feedin' CJ?"

"I tell him about people. And places. And thangs. He keeps my name clean. Ole CJ has just about everybody in the county feedin' him sumpin'. Y'all ain't the only ones."

"Does that mean me and Murven are tidbits?"

"Hell, no. Murven's family," Jesper said, setting his pistol on the table and spinning it with his index finger. "Take a seat. You're making me nervous."

Willem sat down next to Murven, put his elbows on the table, and rested his head in his hands. He figured if Jesper were going to shoot him, it didn't matter whether he was sitting or standing. Jesper looked a little tipsy, so he had a pretty good chance of missing anyway, even at close range.

"Murven said CJ rammed his daddy on purpose."

"Looked that way," Willem said, without lifting his head.

Murven groaned and squirmed in his seat. He started heaving and grabbed Willem's arm.

"Dammit, Murven," Willem said. He looked at Jesper, who grinned and pointed to the front door.

"I'm a'ight," Murven said, between heaves. Willem yanked him out of the chair, spilling the mason jar half-full of shine in Murven's hand, and pulled him out the front door. Murven stumbled down the steps, dropped to his knees and puked.

Jesper stepped out the front door and said, "You better clean him up before Peggy gits here."

"Peggy?" Willem said.

"Murven called her while you were sleeping."

Murven pushed himself to his knees and wiped the puke from his lips. Willem slapped the back of his head, causing him to drop onto all fours and start puking again. Jesper staggered down the steps, waving his gun and fighting to keep his balance. At the bottom of the steps, he pointed with the gun and said, "Here comes Peggy."

Peggy steered her red Miata with the chipped paint and duct-taped convertible top around the mattress pile and parked behind the pickup. After checking her messages, she tossed her phone in the passenger seat, grabbed her camera and shot video of Murven as he puked before getting out of the car.

"I knew you two would be callin' me." She aimed her camera at Willem. "Where y'all wanna do this?"

"We can't do no damn interview," Willem said.

"You can't back out now. Murven made a deal with me. I got exclusive rights to your story."

"Yep," Jesper said, as he plopped down on the steps. "I'm in it, too."

"Why the hell do you wanna be in the interview, Jesper? You want Sheriff Happy to know you were hidin' me and Murven?"

"He ain't gonna know," Murven said, pulling Willem's arm to get to his feet. "We wrote a script."

"We're gonna make it look like it's all a coincidence," Jesper said. "That way I can help y'all and give CJ some tidbits."

"What?" Willem processed what he'd just heard. "Did y'all tell Peggy about the tidbits?"

"Sugar, I've known about CJ and his tidbits long before any of this happened."

"That's part of the deal I negotiated," Murven said. "We give Peggy exclusive rights and she tells us everything she knows."

"And Jesper?" Willem asked.

"He gits to be on the news," Murven said, winking at Jesper and heaving again.

Willem guided Murven to the Miata and leaned him against the hood. He turned to Peggy, pushed the camera out of his face and said, "You first."

"Nope. Interview first, hun."

"Actually," Murven said, swaying on his feet, "we never discussed the order."

"Yeah, so talk, Peggy," Jesper said.

Peggy cleaned her camera lens as she strolled behind her Miata. She popped the trunk and pulled out her tripod. "Let's rehearse," she said.

Jesper teetered to his feet and pointed his gun at Peggy. "Talk. Now."

"Oh, please, Jesper," she said. "You're so drunk you couldn't hit a mountain of shit in Willem's barn."

Jesper turned his gun towards the Miata and shot out the right front headlight. Murven, who had been sprawled out over the hood, rolled off the side and took cover under the car. Willem froze. Peggy dropped her camera and tripod and took cover behind him.

Jesper grabbed Willem's t-shirt, pulled him out of the way, and put the tip of the gun on Peggy's forehead.

"CJ exchanges favors for tidbits," Peggy said.

"We know that already," Jesper said, pressing the pistol into her forehead.

"He makes a deal with pretty much anybody who gits arrested. Most people just tell 'im a bunch'a bullshit and he leaves them alone," Peggy said. Jesper spit and lowered the gun to his side.

"Anybody important feeding him tidbits?" Willem asked.

"I can't say for sure, but I think Poot's one of his informants"

"What's he got on Poot?" Willem said.

"I'm not sure. I think it has something to do with all the real estate he owns. That's all I know."

"I know you know more than that," Willem said.

Peggy looked at the gun in Jesper's hand, rubbed her brow and said, "Willard and Walmer are up to sumpin' with Commissioner Bristol. Sumpin' to do with Poot."

Murven crawled out from under the Miata and said, "What the hell they got against Poot?"

"I can't say exactly, but whatever it is, they don't

want him buyin' your family's property, Willem. Don't ask me why."

"How do you know all this shit?" asked Willem.

"I can't reveal my sources. I'm a journalist. I got integerty," Peggy said, as she glanced at Jesper's pistol. "I'll die before I name anybody." Peggy straightened up and raised her chin while sucking to adjust her teeth.

Willem looked at Jesper, who shrugged and raised his pistol at Peggy. "A'ight," Willem said, stepping between Jesper and Peggy. "Put the camera on me."

Peggy turned up her nose at Jesper, picked up her camera, blew on the lens, and aimed it at Willem.

"I didn't do shit," Willem said. "I'm innocent. There's your interview."

"Wait a minute," Jesper said. "What about me?"

"That's take one," Peggy said, as she fidgeted with the buttons on her camera.

Willem took off his cap and scratched his head as he scoped out the trailer park. He put his cap back on, bent the brim, then steadied Murven against the Miata. As he did, he spotted Peggy's phone in the passenger seat. He looked back at Peggy, then at Jesper, who was spinning his pistol and watching Peggy reset her camera. Willem jutted his hip, causing Murven to fall to the side. As he caught

R.D. SMITH

Murven, he reached his hand into the car and snatched the phone. After balancing Murven, he twisted around and slipped the phone in his back pocket.

"Okay, Jesper. Stand next to Murven," Willem said. "Peggy, you stand in front of 'em and act like you're asking some questions. I'll take your camera and do the filmin'. Hand me your gun, Jesper, so it's not in the shot."

Peggy passed Willem the camera and adjusted her teeth as she positioned herself next to Murven. Jesper leaned against the Miata and put his arm around Murven. He flipped his pistol in his hand and grasped the barrel. He hesitated, looking at Willem with squinted eyes, then handed over the gun, grip first.

Willem backed away as he looked around the trailer park for onlookers. Jesper's eyes widened as Willem raised the gun and pointed it at him. "Where're the keys to your car, Jesper?"

"In the ignition. Nobody's dumb enough to steal my ride."

Willem sidestepped to the rear of the Miata. Jesper shouted, "Wooooo!" as he lunged towards Willem and jumped over the rear end of the car, kicking his feet out for a dropkick. Willem twisted his shoulders as he hopped to the side. Jesper's feet

82

kicked the air and his arms flailed as he stretched out straight. His head slammed into the trunk and his body went limp. He dropped to the ground and didn't move.

"Holy shit," Murven said, grabbing Peggy's shoulders for balance.

"You comin'?" Willem asked.

Murven let go of Peggy and stumbled over to Willem. "I guess so. Jesper's gonna be pissed."

Willem put the camera strap over his shoulder and slid the pistol into the back of his jeans. "Go before he wakes up," he said to Peggy.

"Give me my camera, sugar."

Willem reached his arm behind his back and shook his head. Peggy looked into his exhausted eyes and knew he meant business. She scurried to her car, revved the engine, and without closing the door, tore out of the trailer park.

"I'll drive," Murven said, as Willem lugged him to Jesper's GTO.

Willem leaned to the side, propping Murven on his hip, and opened the passenger door. With a grunt, he swung Murven in the seat and slammed the door. He looked at Jesper, still unconscious on the ground, as he hustled around the car. He jumped in the driver's seat and felt for the keys. Jesper told the truth. Willem twisted the key and the GTO roared to a start. He pulled the seat closer, wrapped his fingers around the steering wheel, checked one last time to make sure Jesper was still out cold, and raced out of the trailer park.

"What's the plan?" Murven asked, over the rumble of the engine.

"Lay low," Willem said, as he checked the rear view mirror, relieved no one was behind them.

Murven leaned his head against the window and said, "You know he's gonna come after us now." His eyes rolled back in his head and he passed out.

Willem gripped the wheel, stood on the gas and said, "Dang."

## Chapter Nine

Deputy CJ read through his story one last time and posted it on the county newspaper's blog. He'd been reinstated as a reporter on the condition that he could only post on the blog, which averaged ten hits per day. Better than nothing. His own blog averaged zero hits per day. CJ's plan to leverage the murders into a crime novel depended on the success of his first-hand account of the investigation. He reported the facts as they were documented in the police report. He only embellished the description of the bodies in the BFF—he needed to paint a picture in words for the readers—and the daring escape by the two violent, possibly armed and dangerous fugitives. Even journalists had some artistic license. To avoid biased reporting, he added his own opinion and speculations as to who the killer may be in italics at the bottom of the story.

Sheriff Happy burst through the door and stomped over to CJ.

"Both cars totaled," he said. "You're off drivin'."

"But deddy! I have to drive! I can't do my job without a vehicle."

"You can't do your job period, son. You're on foot patrol until I change my mind."

"Can I at least git my things outta the car? All my notebooks are in there. I got official documents I need, too."

"Walk over and git it," the sheriff said, as he slammed his office door.

CJ logged out of the blog and checked his phone, wondering why no one had called or texted him with any tidbits. He stood and stretched, with his head tilted towards the sheriff's office. Maybe he could snap up a few tidbits if his daddy was on the phone. But nothing to hear.

CJ closed his laptop and headed out the door. He turned right out of the office and walked towards the garage. As he passed by the diner, he saw Ray Carson in the window booth, sipping on coffee and reading the newspaper. Ray caught a glimpse of CJ and raised the newspaper, blocking his face. The deputy paused outside the window and watched Ray for a moment, but the paper didn't move. CJ shrugged it off, put his hands in his pockets and ambled towards the garage. Ray's tidbits never were very good anyway.

As CJ strolled down the street, he whistled and shifted his eyes from left to right. Jack Dawson, the owner of the hardware store, was sweeping the sidewalk in front of his shop. The deputy pulled his hands out of his pockets, stepped off the curb and jaywalked across the street.

Jack straightened up, took the broom in his right hand and darted inside, putting the "Closed" sign in the window as he shut the door. CJ spun around in the middle of the street, checking to see if anyone saw, then walked on.

Ray and Jack were small-time snitches. CJ needed big hitters. With the murders and the escape, somebody had to be talking about something. He had some time, so he turned right instead of going left towards the garage. He took out his pocket notebook and made a few notes as he approached Poot's office. He lingered out front for a moment, tapped his pen on his leg, and went inside.

"Hey, Sandy. I need to see Poot."

"He ain't here, CJ," Sandy said, without looking up from her computer.

"I know he's here. I can hear him in there, fartin'. Now, tell him I'm here."

"Just go in," Sandy said. "He's expecting you. We saw ya loitering through the window." CJ tapped his pen on Sandy's desk as he passed and sauntered into Poot's office.

"Hey, Pete. Heard you had a truck get stolen last night."

"I done talked to your daddy. I don't know shit about shit."

"Come on now, Poot. It's me you're talkin' to. We have an agreement."

"Yeah, well, I'm gettin' tired of this agreement. I don't know anything about what's goin' on with Willem."

CJ tapped his pen on Poot's desk. Maybe it was too early to press him for information. Some tidbits get better when they stew for a while.

"A'ight. But if you hear anything, you call me first. Got it?"

"Yeah, I got it. Now I need to git back to work."

CJ backed out of the office and pulled the door shut. He tipped his hat to Sandy and walked out of the building, checking his phone as the door shut behind him. Still no calls and no texts. As he walked towards the garage, he scrolled through his old messages—maybe he'd missed something—and kept his eyes peeled for opportunity. He looked down the empty street and wondered what was causing him to lose his grip on his sources. His tidbits were getting dry and crusty before the murders. Now they'd disappeared completely.

CJ entered the garage and walked to the service counter. Chester Darwin, the garage owner and life-long friend of Sheriff Happy, sat reading a hot rod magazine.

"Go away, CJ." Chester flipped a page in the magazine.

"But—"

"Your daddy told me to keep you away from the vehicles. Now git."

"Deddy knows I'm here. He told me I could get my notebooks and stuff."

Chester picked up the phone as he pointed to the bench in the waiting area. CJ took off his hat and sat down. He felt like he was in the principal's office in high school, waiting for his daddy to come bail him out of trouble. Chester hung up the phone and said, "A'ight. Make it fast. What the hell stinks so bad in your car anyhow, boy?"

"Uh, I don't know," CJ said, rubbing his chin. "Um, a prisoner probably pissed in the back seat or sumpin'. Guess I'm just used to the smell." CJ grinned at Chester for a moment, then turned and walked out the door to the garage.

He stood at the door, taking in the sight of the two totaled squad cars. He jiggled the handle to make sure the door closed all the way, then advanced towards the nearest vehicle. As he bent over, he rubbed his hand along the rear quarter panel of his daddy's squad car. He gulped when he realized how hard he had rammed the vehicles. The damage hadn't seemed so bad in the heat of the moment the night before.

As he slid his hand over the crinkled metal, his eyes shifted to his squad car. He smiled when he saw the trunk crushed like an accordion. His car had spun into a ditch, rear end first, preventing him from getting to the trunk at the accident scene. The severity of the damage had also prevented access by anyone else. He spun around and spotted a crowbar leaning against the wall. He picked it up, bounced it in his hands to test the weight, then tried to spin it like a baton, dropping it on the floor. He snatched it up as he watched for Chester to come through the door. Satisfied that Chester wouldn't walk in, CJ put his right leg on the bumper, placed the tip of the crow bar near the trunk latch and pushed down with both hands. The trunk popped open as CJ and the crowbar crashed to the ground.

"Don't be breaking shit!" Chester shouted, without getting up from the counter.

"It's all good!" CJ rubbed his knee as he got to his feet. He slid the crowbar back towards the wall with his foot. He yanked on the trunk lid to open it, keeping an eye on the door, and ducked his head inside. He winced as a stench wafted past his face. Chester wasn't kidding.

His box of case files had spilled in the crash and scattered throughout the trunk. As he pushed the papers to one side, he raised his eyebrows and noted that the cluttered case files could make a good excuse to delay the investigation. He retrieved his notebooks and stacked them on the garage floor. After checking for Chester again, he lifted the trunk carpet, felt around next to the spare tire and pulled out a white plastic grocery bag.

The smell was almost too much to handle, but he untied the bag and opened it. He turned his head to the side and exhaled as he peered into the bag out of the corner of his eye. Just what he'd figured. The three fingers had congealed and started to decompose. CJ retied the bag and searched the garage for a place to dump the fingers. Nothing. He tightened the knot and twisted the bag into a small ball. As he tried to force the bag into his left pocket, the end burst open, splashing finger jelly on his hand, in his pocket, and down the side of his leg. "Shit, shit, shit," he said, as he finished putting the bag in his pocket. Grabbing the first aerosol can he spotted, he sprayed his pants, not noticing it was engine degreaser until he sat it down to wash his hands. At least it would cover the smell. While drying his hands with the cleanest rag he could find, his phone rang. He glanced at the caller ID and said, "Talk to me, Jesper. Tidbit me."

"They were here, but they left."

"When?"

"Little while ago. Not sure how long. This is my last tidbit, CJ."

"Bullshit. I own you."

"Kiss my ass."

The phone went silent. CJ wiped his greasy phone on his leg, put it in his clean pocket and said, "Dang."

## Chapter Ten

Willem whipped the GTO off the paved road and coasted to a stop in the woods that stretched for miles beyond the highway. He'd driven out to the sticks while Murven slept. As he killed the engine, he gazed over at Murven, then at Peggy's video camera on the dashboard. He'd played the video while driving, but it proved useless. The only footage on it was from Jesper's place that morning.

He reclined his seat as he pulled Peggy's phone from his back pocket and pressed the home button at the base of the phone. "Missed Call: Handy" displayed on the screen. "What the hell?" Willem said to himself. He slid his finger across the screen, and the keypad for the password popped up. Of course, he thought. Peggy was too smart not to have a password. He rested his head against the seat as he tapped in random numbers. No luck. Handy's call was the only lead. Murven, sawing logs and filling the car with moonshine fumes, farted and shifted in his seat. Willem reached over to shake him but decided he wasn't much use hung over. He'd let him sleep until they reached Handy's place.

Howard "Handy" Drucker lived in a rundown trailer park on the county line. Rose Blossom Resort Trailer Park never was a very popular place. Handy's father bought the land with the grand idea of building a trailer park resort community. The land parcel had a small creek that trickled through the center, and Handy's dad planned to dam the creek to create a lake. He'd bought ten trailers and placed them in future prime water front locations. For years, Old Man Drucker marketed Rose Blossom, setting up a booth at the flea market every weekend and passing out flyers. But nobody ever rented a trailer, and Old Man Drucker never got around to building the dam. The stench from the neighboring landfill was too much for people to handle. Handy inherited Rose Blossom, converted it into his own private compound, and later scored his dream job as care-taker of the landfill.

Willem slowed the car when he spotted the faded sign for Rose Blossom. He turned and steered down the bumpy dirt road leading to Handy's place.

A chain-link fence surrounded the property, and the trailers formed a semicircle along the inside perimeter of the fence. Over the tops of the trailers he could see the landfill off in the distance. As he drove through the gate, propped open with a cinder block, he noticed one of the trailers in the middle of the semicircle sat half-buried in a hole. Handy, hunched over with a shovel, stopped working long enough to wave, then went back to tossing dirt around the trailer. Willem honked in reply as he parked the GTO next to Handy's garbage truck.

Murven, startled by the horn, jerked in his seat and blurted out, "What's happenin'?!" He sat up, holding his stomach and trying to clear his cotton-mouth. "Where are we?" he asked. "Is that Handy?"

Willem handed Murven the phone as he slipped Jesper's gun under the front seat. "I'll be damned," Murven said, tossing the phone in Willem's lap. The keypad was still showing, so Willem tried another number combination. Still no luck.

He and Murven walked side-by-side towards Handy, jumping the ditch that used to be the creek, and stopped a few feet from the buried trailer. "What's all this?" Murven said.

"I'm making a bunker," Handy replied, as he scooped up dirt from the pile next to the trailer. "I didn't dig the hole deep enough." He tossed the dirt on the trailer. "I can't git the damn thang back outta the hole, so I'm just gonna cover it."

"What the hell you need a bunker for?" Murven asked, walking around to get a look at the back side of the trailer. All the windows and doors had sheet metal welded over them, and one of the windows in the back had been converted into a trap door.

"Endgame's comin', boys. Why y'all here? Y'all should be gittin' as far away as possible."

"Why'd you call Peggy?" Willem said, exhausted and not in the mood for small talk.

Handy leaned in toward Willem and said, "Conspiracy."

Willem raised his shoulders, unsure what to say. As Murven completed his circle around the trailer, he gave Handy a nod and said, "Conspiracy? You tryin' to get on her YouTube channel or sumpin'?"

"Not right away. Not until my evidence reaches critical mass." Handy stood the shovel upright in the dirt and pushed his oversized glasses up on his nose with his middle finger. "Right now, I supply her info." Handy was the local conspiracy theory expert. "I do her favors now. She does me favors later."

"What kinda info?" Willem asked.

Handy wiped his hands on his blue coveralls, pushed his glasses up and looked over Willem's shoulder toward the gate. "Come with me," he said.

Willem and Murven followed Handy to the trailer next to the bunker. They walked up the steps single-file, with Murven bringing up the rear. The trailer was full of papers, some in stacks on the floor and some filed in boxes, all organized and labeled with yellow sticky notes. Murven slapped Willem on the back and said, "Critical mass."

"We ain't got time for this shit, Handy," Willem said. "Please just tell me what the hell you're doing with Peggy."

"When the time's right, she's gonna make my evidence go viral."

"Why don't you just get a blog or your own YouTube or sumpin'? You don't need her," Murven said.

"Hell, no. I wouldn't last a day online. The FBI would be all over me. I don't even own a computer. I'm analog. Old school. Paper's my Zen, boys." Handy cleaned the dirt out of his teeth with his tongue as he looked back and forth between Willem and Murven. "Y'all don't git it. Peggy's gonna be my patsy."

Handy tiptoed through the piles of paper and squeezed past the boxes, holding his glasses on his face as he bent to read the sticky notes. "Three different states in the region, soon to be four, dump in this landfill." He thumped one of the stacks, then spun to face Willem and Murven. "That's five states worth of paper trail. This landfill might as well be a gold mine."

"You recyclin' or sumpin'?" Murven asked.

"No, my naïve friend." Handy reached into the nearest box. "They throw away information. Nobody pays attention to what's on paper these days. They shred some thangs but not enough. Everybody's worried about hackers. People think nobody goes through the trash anymore. That's how I stay under the radar." He pulled a stained envelope out of the box. "See this? This is an unfinished thank-you card written by a U.S. senator that I won't name at this time."

"What's that prove?" Murven said, inspecting the card in Handy's hand.

"He made a mistake on the card. He probably threw it away to start over. But the question is, who is the card to? Why did he make that mistake? Was he nervous?"

"Hold up," Willem said. "I don't care about your conspiracy theories right now. What does Peggy want from you?"

"Oh," Handy said, filing the card back in the box. He pushed his glasses up, looked into Willem's eyes and walked out of the trailer. "Come with me," he said from the bottom of the steps. As they headed towards the bunker, Handy stopped in his tracks, stood with his back to the other two, and stared at the ground. "I like you, Willem. You were always good to me."

At that moment, Willem saw the Handy he knew in high school. The scrawny kid with the big glasses targeted by bullies. Willem had felt a connection with Handy back then. Willem's brothers had tried to bully him, but his predisposition for not taking any shit prevailed, and the other Wisely boys eventually just learned to ignore him. Willem's own experience with bullies led to a moderate friendship with Handy. Though he didn't go out of his way, Willem felt sorry for Handy and stood up for him whenever he could. They never hung out outside of school. For Willem, Handy was a high school acquaintance he'd lost his connection with after graduation. For Handy, Willem was the only best friend he'd ever had.

"I'm sorry," Willem said. "It's just we ain't got much time, Handy."

"I know," Handy said. "I wanna help ya." He turned around, looked at Willem and Murven, then glanced over his shoulder towards the gate. He rubbed his hands on his coveralls as he paced in a small circle. He took a deep breath and exhaled as he said, "Peggy wants to know about Poot."

"Yeah, she thinks he's up to sumpin' with his trailer parks. She told us," Willem said.

"Oh. Well, she asked me to look through his trash. Sure enough, gold mine." Handy exaggerated his pronunciation. "Poot is using the trailer parks and all his real estate," he said, pausing to make sure he had the others attention, "to launder money."

"Bullshit," Willem said.

"No, really. I found shredded documents in his garbage. I pieced together enough of 'em to prove it."

Willem took off his hat and rubbed his head. "That makes sense," Willem said. "That's why he don't give a shit if people pay rent or not. Hot damn."

"Poot's a crook," Murven said, as he spit and reached for his Skoal in his back pocket, forgetting he was out. "Do the murders have anything to do with all that shit?"

"Couldn't tell ya," Handy said, "but I did find new information this morning. That's why I was callin' Peggy."

"What did you find?"

Handy rubbed his hands on his coveralls, took off his glasses and turned away. "Uh, it's best if I show you." He put his glasses on and wiped the sweat off his forehead. He kept his back to Willem and Murven as he waved them toward the bunker.

Willem grabbed Murven's arm and said, "This ain't right."

"Handy ain't right. Let's just see what he found."

Handy stopped and waited beside his shovel. He turned away when Willem made eye contact. Murven walked towards Handy while Willem stayed back.

"Just come on," Murven said, glancing back at Willem, and continued to the bunker.

Willem waited until Murven and Handy were behind the trailer before following. He clenched his jaw as he pulled the shovel out of the ground and turned the corner. Murven was watching as Handy spun the dial on the combination.

"He can't remember the combination," Murven said, grinning and spinning his finger next to his head. Willem relaxed his jaw, dropped the shovel, and stood next to Murven.

The lock clicked and Murven sighed. "Finally." Handy grabbed the handle on the sheet metal hatch and lifted it open.

"This is where I keep my most sensitive documents," he said. "Check it out."

Murven squeezed through the hatch, climbed down the wobbly stepladder, and shouted, "It's dark as hell down here!"

Willem bent to look inside. As his head passed

through the entrance, Handy kicked Willem in his butt, and he crashed to the floor of the bunker. The hatch closed.

Willem shouted, "Goddammit, Handy! What the hell are you doin'?!" Murven raced up the stepladder and pushed the hatch, but it wouldn't open. He jumped down and lifted Willem up off the ground.

Handy tapped on the door and shouted, "Just so you know, I ain't callin' Sheriff Happy."

"Handy!" Willem shouted, holding his back with his right hand and his head with his left. "Let us outta here, damn it!"

Murven bent over, picked up Willem's cap, and handed it to him. Willem slapped the cap out of Murven's hand, kicked the wall and said, "Dang."

# Chapter Eleven

Peggy checked her YouTube hits and read through CJ's blog article one last time before turning off her computer. He'd actually kept it fairly accurate and only speculated at the end, like all good journalists do. She thought to herself that she and CJ might actually make a good team if he wasn't such a shithead. But that was never going to happen. She would never let CJ steal her thunder. A killer loose in the county was the perfect opportunity for one of them to gain exposure, and it sure as hell wasn't going to be Deputy Dipshit.

The call from Murven in the middle of the night had forced her to change her plans for the day. She'd lost her camera, one of those dumbasses had her phone, and she nearly got shot in the head. None of that was on her to-do list. Oh hell, oh well. To be a successful news correspondent, she had to take risks. If the big-time journalists on TV could report from war zones, surely she could navigate safely through the trailer park scene. When competing for the scoop, shit happened, and part of Peggy—a big part she'd always kept buried inside—felt exhilarated by it.

She had to put the morning behind her and get on with her plans. She spread her equipment out on the kitchen table and took inventory. She untangled the bundle of red and green wires and rolled them up again. Not sure which she would need, she confirmed that she had one Phillips-head and one flathead screwdriver. She put the wires and the screwdrivers in her purse and chucked a roll of duct tape and electrical tape in on top. She picked up the mini-cassette recorder, loaded a tape and flipped it on. "Test, one two. Test, one two," she said. She played the tape back. The voice-activated recording function worked fine. She rewound the tape and packed it with the rest of her gear. She adjusted her teeth as she closed her purse and propped it by the door.

Peggy looked at herself in the mirror and took pride in how far her investigative journalist spy skills had come. A year ago, she'd seen some of the kids in the trailer park playing with toy spy gear. That same day, she headed straight to the toy store and bought them out of spy toys. She'd learned to strip the toys down to just the microphone. After a little practice on the neighbors, the next thing she knew, she'd bugged Poot's office. Her bug couldn't record anything and she couldn't hear the other end of the phone conversation, but she'd pieced together that Poot was laundering money through his real estate. She dabbed bright red lipstick on her thin lips, checked for smudges on her teeth, and smiled. Her new bug was so much better.

As she brushed her graying hair, she joked to herself that she was a straight-A student at YouTube University. After several hours of watching how-to videos, she'd learned everything she needed to know about bugging a phone. With her new bug, she could place it, record both sides of the conversation and pick it up later. No more hiding and listening. Once her own YouTube channel took off, which it was sure to do after the murders, she planned to buy high-tech remote listening equipment. For now, her homemade bug for Commissioner Bristol's phone would do the trick. She was dying to find out why the commissioner didn't want Poot to buy the Wisely property.

She pulled back her hair and lifted her chin to stretch out the wrinkles on her neck. She regretted not taking better care of herself in her younger days. The past is over, she told herself. Now she was discovering hidden skills and acting on urges she had felt all her life. She lowered her arms and stared at herself for a moment, wondering what life would have been like had she discovered her latent talents earlier. She snapped out of her daydream and cocked her head when she heard a truck turning into the trailer park. The sound of the engine grew louder as the truck pulled up to her trailer. Peggy made her way to the window and listened. When the brakes gasped, she yanked the curtains open and saw Handy climbing out of his garbage truck. She opened the window and hollered, "What the hell are you doing here, sugar?"

"Critical mass! I've reach critical mass!" Handy said, raising his hands in the air and shouting over the truck engine.

"I thought you said it'd be a couple years 'fore that happened."

"I thought so, but it's all comin' together. Nexus! We gotta git to my place!" Handy shouted, pacing in front of his truck. "I need to teach ya all the details. It'll take a few days. Bring a change of clothes."

"I can't go out there now, hun. I got things I need to do."

"It's a sign." Handy put his hands on the

windowsill. "The murders. Willem and Murven. It's all a sign."

"What about Willem and Murven?"

"They showed up at my place. I got 'em locked in my bunker."

"Good lord, Handy." Peggy closed her window, grabbed her gear, and raced out the door.

"You gotta release the evidence now," Handy said, as he followed Peggy to her car. "Willem and Murven are martyrs!"

"Damn, sugar. Don't go killin' anybody just yet." Peggy tossed her bag in her car. "Keep 'em there. I gotta take care of some business, then I'll come see ya."

"But wait! I know who Poot's money laundering partner is."

Peggy, halfway in the driver's seat, pulled her head up and looked at Handy over the convertible top. "Who is it?"

"It's Wilton Wisely."

"Well, don't that beat all. Can you prove it?"

"Yep," Handy said, nodding and pushing up his glasses.

"A'ight, sugar. I'll be there soon."

Peggy sat down and pointed Handy towards his garbage truck through the windshield. Handy climbed in his truck and maneuvered his way out of the trailer park. Peggy bounced her leg and tapped on the steering wheel while she waited for Handy to clear out of her way. She waved to the deputy posted at the entrance and raced to town, pushing her Miata to the limit. With the manhunt and her own history with the police, she wasn't concerned about being pulled over. Shortly after she started her YouTube channel, she discovered that recording traffic stops, creating a scene and posting the video caused her hits to spike. Sheriff Happy caught on and ordered his deputies not to pull Peggy over unless she was a threat to herself or the safety of others. She had inadvertently created her own sort of diplomatic immunity.

She parked her car down the road from the commissioner's office and waited. Twisting her head around, she looked to see if anyone noticed her, but nobody was paying attention. It wasn't unusual for the folks in town to see Peggy sitting in her car ready to pounce on a news story. Hiding in plain sight, Peggy thought. One of her favorite spy skills. Peggy slid down in her seat when she saw Commissioner Bristol walk out of his office with his assistant, Nancy. Peggy slid her teeth in and out as she watched them walk towards the tanning salon. The commissioner tanned during his lunch break, and Nancy always had lunch at the diner. Peggy checked her watch. She had about an hour to complete her mission.

She grabbed her gear and strolled down the street. At the bottom of the steps, she paused to check for onlookers. The coast was clear. She walked up the steps backwards, shifting her eyes from left to right. She reached back and felt for the door handle, keeping her eyes on the street. She pushed the door open, backed into the office, and peered out the window as the door closed. Easy as pie, she thought, as she grinned and straightened her teeth.

She could smell coconut tanning oil from the office corridor. The scent made her dizzy as she slipped inside the commissioner's waiting room. As she made her way across the room, she looked at the photos of classic cars on all four walls and the racing trophies in the corner trophy case. The commissioner's father, Thurman Bristol, had owned several car dealerships and a NASCAR regional series race team. Terry took pride in that part of his family history. Thurman had also owned several back-room gambling establishments, got busted by the feds, and died in prison. Terry, not so proud of that family story, sold the dealerships and the race team in an effort to differentiate himself from his father. After graduating from college, Terry went into local politics. His political career plateaued at Chief County

Commissioner, but rumor was he was cleaning up the county in an effort to position himself to run for governor. Peggy thought about digging for evidence to substantiate the rumor, but that was another mission for another day.

The door to the commissioner's private office creaked and the smell of coconut tanning oil grew stronger as Peggy proceeded. She closed the door behind her and put her bag on the commissioner's oak desk. In her scouting visits, Peggy had bullshitted her way into the commissioner's office on several occasions; she'd already located the phone jack in the wall next to the desk. She took hold of the desk, lifted with her back and pulled with all her strength. The desk inched away from the wall, and after four big tugs, she had space to access the wall jack.

She squatted down and wiped the dust off the housing as she checked the screws. After standing and stretching her back for a moment, she put her bag on the floor and pulled out her Phillips-head screwdriver. As she twisted the screws, her heart raced with excitement. She loved the way she felt in these moments. Dust fell on the carpet as she pulled the wall jack from the wall. She inspected the wiring, which looked just like she'd expected, and followed the steps she'd learned from her training videos. She connected the red wire to the red and the green to the green, fed all the wiring back into the wall and replaced the housing. After connecting the bug to the mini-cassette recorder, she wrapped the wires with electrical tape. Peggy clicked her teeth with satisfaction.

She picked up the receiver and listened for a dial tone. So far, so good. Losing her cell phone had complicated her plan to test the recorder, but at that moment she felt grateful to whichever idiot had lifted it. Improvising gave her butterflies and the tickle in her belly made her chuckle. She took a deep breath and calmed herself before heading back towards the waiting room to use Nancy's phone.

As she reached for the doorknob, she heard the door to the corridor open. She pressed her ear to the door and listened. Peggy's heart raced, adrenaline pumping through her body. She fought back a smile, realizing she needed to make a move. She stood still and listened, holding her breath, not sure what to do if the commissioner's office door opened. She exhaled when she heard the desk chair squeak and the sound of Nancy typing.

Peggy stepped to the desk with long, silent strides, on her toes like an out-of-shape ballet dancer, and dropped down on her knees next to her bug. She removed the duct tape from her purse and rolled out a strip, inch by inch, noting to herself to find a quicker and more efficient method to keep the duct tape from croaking during missions. She stuck the strip on the mini-cassette recorder and taped it under the desk. As she packed her gear and got to her feet, she listened as Nancy continued to type away. Peggy grabbed the sides of the desk and held her breath as she lifted and pushed with her hip. On her last push, the desk bumped the wall and the typing stopped. Peggy ducked under the desk and listened. After a moment, she heard the typing resume and bolted from under the desk.

She picked up her purse, sucking her teeth as the screwdrivers clanged inside, and tiptoed to the window. While looking over her shoulder towards the door, she lifted the window and then the screen. She chucked her purse out the window and climbed through, dropping to the ground in a row of large bushes on the side of the building. She spun around and closed the window and the screen. After peeping in the window for one final check, she picked up her purse, adjusted her teeth and said, "Dang."

# Chapter Twelve

Handy's bunker made for a crappy prison. After only a few minutes of feeling around in the dark, Murven found a loose piece of sheet metal and kicked it off the window. With Handy gone, Willem and Murven had free rein to sift through Handy's conspiracy evidence. Boxes and papers from floor to ceiling filled three of the trailers at Rose Blossom. They started in the trailer Handy had taken them to earlier, searching for the information Handy meant to share with Peggy. Murven passed boxes down from the stack while Willem skimmed the papers and Post-It Notes, unable to crack the nonsensical code and conspiracy terminology Handy used to organize his findings.

"Holy shit," Murven said. "This box is labeled 'Wisely Fire.'"

Willem tossed the papers in his hands on the floor and climbed the boxes to get to Murven. He snatched the box out of Murven's hand, causing Murven to lose balance and fall into the corner. Willem kicked the paper and boxes at his feet to the side and dropped to his knees, ripping the lid as he tore into the box.

"It's empty," he said, turning the box over and shaking it.

The rumble of Handy's garbage truck pulling through the gate rattled the trailer. Willem stretched his neck and peeked out the vibrating windows. "He's back," Willem said. "He's headed for the bunker." Willem squeezed through the boxes to get to the door. Murven jumped and laid himself out over the top of the boxes that had him pinned in the corner. He slid to the floor and rolled to his feet behind Willem. They tossed boxes to the side and pushed the door open.

When they stepped out on the porch, Handy stopped in his tracks. He thrust his arms out to the side, tilted his head, then broke into a sprint. His hips wiggled and his knees flew up to his chest as he ran towards the bunker.

"Handy! Stop!" Willem cried, as he and Murven leaped off the porch in pursuit.

Handy swung his arms in giant circles as he corned around the bunker and headed for the landfill. He climbed the mound of dirt behind the bunker and jumped into the air at the top. Rotating his body in mid-air, he slid down the backside of the dirt pile and under the fence. After clearing the fence, he somersaulted to his feet, yanked a rope hanging from the nearest tree, sending a couple hundred pounds of landfill debris crashing to the ground, and hauled ass into the maze he'd built. Without looking back once, Handy had perfectly executed the evasive protocol he practiced daily in the event of a raid by the FBI, CIA, NSA or any other government or non-governmental entity.

Willem and Murven stopped at the top of the dirt pile to look out over the fallen debris and into the maze.

"There ain't no way we'll find him in that shit. Even without that damn maze," Willem said. "Let's keep searching the files."

They made their way back to the trailer and continued sifting through Handy's files. Nothing made sense. Most of the documents looked like trash to the untrained eye. "You see anything about the fire?" Murven asked, as he chucked a box in the corner.

"Nah. I don't see anything about anything,"

Willem said. "If Handy has evidence about some giant conspiracy, I couldn't tell ya what it is."

Murven nodded and did a double-take out the window. "Guess who just pulled up?"

Willem looked around Murven and out the window. "Let's go," he said, as he headed out the door. Peggy's red Miata pulled up next to the garbage truck and Peggy hopped out with a grin on her face. "Well, hey there," she said. "I thought Handy had y'all locked up or some shit."

"Go away," Willem said, pointing to the trailer park entrance.

"You still wanna do an interview?" Murven asked.

"Oh, honey, the interview ship done sailed. Don't wanna look like an accomplice."

"Dammit," Murven mumbled under his breath.

"I came out here to talk Handy into lettin' y'all go." Peggy put her hands on her hips and eyeballed the trailer park.

"Bullshit," Willem said.

"Think what you want, sugar. I was also hopin' we could make a new deal."

"We ain't on no media tour," Willem said. "We're tryin' to clear our names. Unless you can help with that, we ain't interested."

"What can I do to make you trust me?" Peggy put her hand on Willem's shoulder.

Willem pulled away, reached into his pocket and shoved Peggy's phone in her face.

"Lemme call Cindy. Start with that."

Peggy took the phone, looked at Willem for a moment, keyed in her password, and handed it back to Willem.

He tapped in the number, keeping his eyes on Peggy. She crossed her arms and watched him as he waited for Cindy to pick up.

"I ain't doin' no damn interview, Peggy. Quit callin'!" Cindy shouted over the phone.

"Wait! It's me!"

"Willem? Thank God. Are you OK? Where are you?"

"I'm fine. Probably best if you don't know too much. I'm safe," Willem said, raising his eyebrows at Murven. "What's happenin' there?"

"Sheriff's tearing our trailer apart. Goin' through our bank account and askin' me shitloads of questions about your brothers."

"What the hell do they wanna know about my brothers?"

"They're asking me about money transfers and a bunch'a shit I don't know anything about. Sumpin's goin' on."

"Money transfers. What the hell?"

"I don't know. It don't make sense. Why do you have Peggy's phone?"

"It's a long story. Better not talk much. Just wanted to let ya know I'm safe. Tell Luna Murven's all good, too."

"But... OK. Be careful. Love you."

"Love you, too." Willem stared at the phone until the display light faded. Peggy reached for it, but Willem stuffed it into his back pocket.

"What's the word?" Murven asked, as he sat on the hood of the Miata.

"It sounds like they think I'm up to sumpin' with my brothers."

Willem crossed his arms and leaned against the GTO. He watched Peggy as she stared at the ground and fidgeted with her teeth. Peggy took a deep breath, locked eyes with Willem and said, "I can't promise I can clear your names, but I can promise I won't turn you in."

Her tone changed. "You know I have my sources and you know I can find things out. But it's not enough. I need y'all to help me git the scoop on CJ."

Willem crumpled his eyebrows, taken off guard by the seriousness in Peggy's voice. Her eyes had a darkness he'd never seen. He looked over at Murven, then back at Peggy. "What the hell does that mean?"

"It means these murders are my ticket to the big time, sugar. Ain't no way I'm lettin' CJ steal this from me." Peggy's voice lightened, but the darkness in her eyes remained.

"You and CJ are damn near crazy. There ain't gonna be no books, no movies, no nothin'. All that's gonna happen is me and Murven are gonna wind up in prison for life."

"This is bigger than you think," Peggy said in a low voice. She paced in front of the GTO and gazed off towards the bunker. After a moment, she spun towards Willem. "Lemme see my phone, sugar." Willem bounced himself off the car and put his hands in his front pockets.

"I can help you," she said, as she held out her hand.

Willem pulled the phone from his back pocket and slapped it in Peggy's palm. She held it close to her body and her fingers danced as she quickly tapped in a series of numbers. She scrolled through the pictures, stopped on a photo, and looked up at Willem. As she tucked the phone against her chest, she said, "These were emailed to me. I don't know who sent 'em, so don't ask." She held the phone to Willem's face. "Recognize this place?"

Willem looked closely and said, "Uh, yeah, that's the hobo jungle." He looked up at Peggy, then back at the phone. Peggy swiped to the next picture and Willem's eyes nearly popped out of his head. He grabbed the phone and said, "How did you get these?"

"What is it?" Murven asked, bounding off the Miata.

"It's Wilbur talkin' to a bunch'a hobos." Willem flipped through more of the pictures. "Where did you git these?" he said, not taking his eyes off the photo.

"I don't know. I started gettin' 'em in my email a couple months ago."

"You knew about this for a couple months?" Willem looked up at Peggy. Her grin had returned.

"I knew Wilbur was hanging out with hobos, sugar. That's all I knew. I didn't make a connection to the murders until I read CJ's article."

Willem glanced at Murven, who shrugged in confusion. "Why did you show me these?" He thumped his finger on the phone. "Whaddya tryin' to git outta me?"

"I done told ya. I want y'all to be my sources so I can git the scoop on CJ. I showed you those pictures to git you to trust me."

Willem studied Peggy's face, searching for her angle. "Come clean. What else do you know?"

Peggy crossed her arms and fixed her eyes on

Willem. "Give me my phone and camera back and I'll tell ya everything I know, sugar."

Willem reached through the car window, grabbed the camera and handed it to Peggy. He turned the phone in his hand. It had already switched back to the lock screen. "What's the password?"

"Uh, I forgot." Peggy rubbed her temples. "My memory must be going."

Willem bit his lip and tossed her the phone. "So talk."

Peggy smiled as she put the phone in her pocket. "I just learned from Handy that Wilton is Poot's money laundering partner."

"Wilton?" Willem took off his cap and rubbed his head. "That kinda makes sense." He slid his cap on and bent the brim. "Is my whole family corrupt? Do you know more than you told us about Willard and Walmer?"

"No, but I'm working on it, sugar."

"And you'll tell us when you do know?" Willem said, raising his eyebrows.

"Well, of course I will, hun. As long as we come to an agreement."

Willem looked at Peggy, hoping for her to reveal something, but he couldn't see through her poker face. "Let's go, Murven," he said. He slung the GTO door open and sat in the driver's seat.

"I hope you have a plan, hun. You might end up needin' me."

"Got a plan," Willem said, looking at Murven and directing him to the passenger seat with his thumb. Murven raised his hands as he walked past Peggy and got in the car.

"By the way," Willem said, as he slammed the door, "do you know why Handy has a file on the fire?"

"Handy has a file on the fire?" Peggy asked. "Where?"

Willem pointed to the bunker. Peggy knocked on the side of the car and took off.

"Good luck," she said over her shoulder. "Be in touch."

Willem cranked the engine and felt around under the seat. He looked at Murven as he cocked the pistol over the steering wheel. Murven slid down in his seat, put his knees on the dashboard and said, "Dang."

## Chapter Thirteen

Deputy CJ sniffed as he raised his hand to knock on the door. He could still smell the degreaser on his hands, but at least it covered the odor of decomposing fingers. His mind wandered for moment as he congratulated himself for his own efficiency. After his visit to the garage, he'd dumped the fingers in the sewage drain, as they were mostly jelly anyway, and taken his pants to the dry cleaner for a rush job. His mind drifted back to reality as he realized he still didn't have permission from his daddy to drive. He sniffed again, tapped on the door and waited. He counted to ten and tapped again.

"What?" Sheriff Happy shouted.

Deputy CJ cracked the door, just enough to get his mouth through, and said, "The medical examiner's preliminary report is in, Deddy."

"Is the doc still here?"

"Nah, she emailed the report. She didn't wanna come here. Said she didn't want me asking dumbass questions 'bout ways to kill people. I printed the report for ya." Sheriff Happy was old school. He didn't have a computer in his office.

"What's it say?"

With only his mouth poking through the cracked door, the deputy said, "All four are definitely home-less men in their mid to late forties. Doc said they were most likely killed someplace else and moved to Willem's bio shit fuel after they died. She don't know the cause of death yet."

"Bring it here. She speculate on a cause?"

"Nah," CJ said, as he eased in the door, "she said she needs to run some tests or some shit."

He approached his daddy, who, even seated, was almost as tall as the deputy, and set the report on the desk. "I gotta run some errands, Deddy. I'm gonna take one of the squad cars."

"Like hell you are. You're still off drivin'. Now, git!"

Deputy CJ turned to walk away and paused to look back over his shoulder. His daddy had his head down, reading the report. No use asking again. He made his way out of the office, closing the door behind him. "Shit," he whispered to himself, as he stood outside the door. He checked his phone and closed his laptop as he passed his desk on his way to the door.

The people in town were going about their business despite the murders and the manhunt. He wondered if the people he passed on the street had read his article. He fought the urge to ask, figuring feedback was best when it was spontaneous, and made a mental note to check the newspaper blog later and read the comments. Peggy still didn't have anything more than her interview with Luna on YouTube. He'd reported that the victims were most likely hobos. At least he'd gotten that scoop on the crazy old bat. Once Willem and Murven fed him a few tidbits, he was sure to smoke Peggy in the ratings. To rub it in even more, he was considering paying Cindy a visit to demonstrate to Peggy that, unlike her, he had the authority to coerce information. But Sunny Bluff was too far away to walk. That would have to wait until he got his driving privileges reinstated.

He picked up his pace. He wanted to get to the dry cleaners before the owner, Harry Morgan, closed for the day. As he arrived at the cleaners, he saw Peggy's red Miata pull up in front of the commissioner's office. He jumped inside and watched Peggy through the door.

"Your pants are ready, deputy," Harry said. "I think we got the smell out. You losin' your fingernails or sumpin'? You had a pocket full of 'em."

"Uh, yeah," CJ said, without turning around, "stressed out, I guess. You know what? I'll come back tomorrow."

The deputy opened the door, ran to the side of the building, and waited a second before poking his head around the corner. He watched Peggy as she stood at the front of the commissioner's office and pulled the handle on the locked door. She turned in a circle, checking if anyone was around, then scuttled into the bushes next to the building.

Deputy CJ leaned around the corner, looked left and right, then dashed across the street, holding his cowboy hat on his head. He put his hands in his pockets and whistled while he waited for a moment in front of the commissioner's office. He squatted down and looked into the bushes, but they were too thick to see through. He paced in front of the hedges as he scoped out the street. When he was certain the coast was clear, he pulled his hands out of his pockets, snatched his hat off his head, and squeezed between the bushes and the building. He pounced into the clearing within the bushes, but Peggy wasn't there. He smiled when he saw the window to the commissioner's office open, and slid back into the bushes.

A flashlight beam zipped around in the office and he could hear Peggy's grunts and groans through the open window. When the light went out, CJ took cover deeper in the bushes. Peggy's bag flopped out of the window, and CJ heard the sound of metal jingling as it dropped on the ground. He made a move for the purse, but recoiled when Peggy's right leg stretched out the window, followed by her left. She bounded to the ground and stuck the landing. As she turned and reached to close the window, CJ said, "You're pretty graceful for a worn-out old hag."

Peggy froze, then spun towards the deputy once she'd placed the voice.

"You scared the shit outta me, CJ." Her heart pounded as she took a deep breath and exhaled.

"What the hell are you doin' in there? And don't bullshit me."

"I was gettin' my teeth. I left 'em in there earlier today. Gotta have my teeth," she said, as she adjusted her teeth in her mouth.

"This is the commissioner's office, not the dentist. Try again."

"I ain't tellin' you a damn thang, sugar." Peggy picked up her bag and turned to squeeze through the bushes.

"I caught you red-handed. You're breakin' and enterin'. You wanna talk, or you wanna go to jail?"

Peggy's bag clinked as she slipped it over her shoulder. She looked back at the street then at Deputy CJ. "You ain't gonna do shit, sugar. You take me to jail and I'll tell everybody about you and your tidbits."

The deputy chuckled. "I think everybody already knows. I'm gonna give up on the tidbit thang, anyway. Nobody's talkin' anymore." He reached around his belt and removed his handcuffs from the case.

"Turn around," he said, stepping towards Peggy. "I don't have my car, so I get to walk your ass down the street. I'm gonna love this."

CJ spun his finger in the air, but Peggy didn't budge. She crossed her arms and sucked her teeth. "What do you want?" she said, looking straight at Deputy CJ.

"What's in the bag? I hear shit clankin' around like a toolbox or sumpin'. I know it ain't no denture repair kit."

"I keep a few tools with me in case I get locked outta my car or my trailer. I'm gettin' old, sugar." Peggy tapped on her temple.

"Bullshit," CJ said, as he snatched the bag out of her hand. He opened the bag, looked inside and reached his hand in to feel around. He tossed the bundle of wire on the ground, held up the duct tape, looked at Peggy, then tossed it in the bushes.

"Well, well," he said, as he pulled the tape recorder from the bag, "what do we have here?"

"Oh, I use that to rehearse for my videos. It's just a bunch'a me screwin' up my lines."

The deputy pressed the play button, and Peggy said, "Wait, wait, wait. Before you play that, let's make a deal."

"Hell, no." CJ pressed stop on the tape player. "This must be pretty juicy stuff if you're willing to make a deal with me."

Peggy crossed her arms and looked through the bushes. "Give me the damn tape player or you'll regret it."

"Easy, now. You want me to add threatening an officer to your charges?" CJ smiled. He enjoyed watching Peggy squirm. "I think I'll just have a listen myself. You're free to go." CJ put the recorder in his hat and squeezed back through the bushes. He could hear Peggy cussing to herself as he walked away.

He kept his cool as he moseyed down the street and around the corner. When he was sure he was out of Peggy's sight, he held the recorder to his ear and pressed play. After a minute of static, he heard the commissioner's voice.

"Yeah?"

"Walmer Wisely on the line," his assistant said.

The phone beeped and the commissioner said, "Walmer, what's the word?"

"They're tryin' to search through my bank accounts and business documents, Terry. Willard's, too. What the hell is goin' on? I thought you were gonna handle all this mess."

"I'm doin' what I can. This shit's gettin' outta hand. Happy's talkin' about callin' in the FBI."

"Shit. What're you gonna do? Is Willem goin' down for this?"

"He looks good for it."

"Can you pin it on Poot instead? That'd get him outta our way."

"Maybe. I gotta find the best way to leverage this if I'm gonna win the election. Let's just wait and see what unfolds."

"Yeah, well, I can't wait much longer. Take care of this shit." The phone slammed down and the tape turned to static.

"Hot damn," CJ said out loud. He looked around, but no one was nearby. He kept the recorder to his ear and walked aimlessly as he continued to listen.

"Sherriff Maddocks," the voice on tape said.

"Happy, it's Terry. You call in the FBI yet?

"Not yet. I was waiting for the full report from the medical examiner. Why?"

"Let's hold off on that if we can. Maybe we can sort this thing out ourselves," the commissioner said.

"Depends on what I hear from Doc. It'll be a day or two. I'll let you know."

"A'ight. Thanks." The commissioner's voice cut off and the tape continued to play static.

CJ fast-forwarded the tape, but nothing else was recorded. As he tossed the recorder between his hands, he replayed the conversations in his mind and considered how to best use this new information to his advantage. For a moment, he admired Peggy's initiative, smiling in disbelief at how far she had gone, but he shook it off. She was his competitor. His nemesis. And for now, at least, he was in the lead. He adjusted his cowboy hat, strolled around the corner and said, "Dang."

# Chapter Fourteen

Willem drove an hour past the county line, taking back roads to avoid the manhunt. With only a short stop for fuel, food and Skoal, he and Murven made it to Wilbur's pawnshop as the sun set. The vacant mall lot across the street, which the locals had turned into a used car lot, provided the perfect cover for a stake out. Willem shifted in his seat, balancing his urge to beat the shit out of Wilbur and his curiosity to know what the hell Wilbur was doing with the hobos. Murven's enthusiasm for media opportunities was stronger than ever, and he rehearsed lines to say on the news or on the witness stand, whichever came first.

Business appeared to be slow. Wilbur had a reputation for buying and selling anything people brought to him, but nobody had come or gone since they'd set up surveillance. Light radiated from the pawnshop, the only business open on that stretch of highway, and Wilbur leaned on the glass counter, talking on his cell phone and looking at papers spread over the counter top.

"Hell with this," Willem said, as he pounded the steering wheel.

He opened the door and Murven grabbed his arm. "He ain't gonna tell you jack shit. Even if you do beat the shit out of him."

Willem kept one leg out the door as he considered his options. "This is bullshit." He slammed the door, settled back in his seat and resumed the stake out, watching Wilbur study the papers and talk on the phone. Willem twisted in his seat, scanning the mall and the parking lot, and opened the door. "I'm callin' Peggy," he said, before Murven could snag his arm.

"Really?" Murven asked.

Willem didn't answer as he headed toward the pay phone on the edge of the parking lot. He checked for a dial tone, dialed the number, and kept his eye on Wilbur, still doing a whole bunch of nothing while he waited.

"Hello?" Peggy said.

"You got any news?"

"Hell, no. That little shit CJ done pissed me off."

"What happened?"

"He got to one of my sources," Peggy hollered.

Willem pulled the phone away from his ear. "Are you drunk or sumpin'?"

"I quit drinkin' years ago, sugar. Made me crazy." Peggy paused. "I need you to help me git under CJ's skin. Can you do that for me?"

"How?" Willem looked back to check on Murven, who was packing dip in his lip and mouthing lines.

"Call that little shit and say, 'I know about the fingers.' Say those exact words and hang up. Okay?"

"Yeah, but what does it mean?"

"Don't worry about that. Just say 'I know about the fingers' and that boy will go cuckoo crazy."

"Uh, a'ight," Willem said. "Now?"

"Yeah. Now." Peggy hung up.

Willem looked across the street at Wilbur. Nothing new. He dropped his coins in the slot and dialed the number.

"Sheriff's office," Deputy CJ said.

"It's me."

"Why you callin' me here?" CJ whispered.

"I know about the fingers," Willem said in a monotone.

"What?" CJ shouted.

"I know about the fingers," Willem repeated and slammed the phone on the receiver.

Willem checked the pawnshop and hauled ass to the car. "He's on the move," he said, as he hopped in the driver's seat. He pointed to Wilbur, who grabbed a gun from the display case and turned out the lights.

"Let's do it," Murven said, drumming on the dashboard. They watched Wilbur lock up the pawnshop and crank his red '84 Corvette.

Murven slipped in a fresh dip, winked, and flipped a homemade switch mounted to the dashboard of the GTO, disconnecting the circuit to the brake lights. Like all good bootleggers, Jesper had rigged his car to be invisible at night. Willem started the engine, turned onto the highway and followed Wilbur's taillights in the distance. The long stretch of isolated highway made for easy stalking.

After several miles, Wilbur's headlights swiveled to the right and vanished in the darkness. Willem pulled the GTO onto the shoulder and crawled along, cautious not to approach too quickly. Once they'd reached Wilbur's turnoff, Murven pointed out the window and said, "Gravel road."

Willem muscled the steering wheel to the right, and two sets of headlights bobbed around the curve in the distance. "Dammit," he said, shifting into reverse and backing off the shoulder. The shocks squeaked as the GTO bounced into the field, the overgrown grass engulfing the car. Willem killed the engine, looked over at Murven and pointed upward. They climbed out the windows and stretched out on the roof of the car.

The first truck slowed to a stop at the intersection. Wilbur sat in the driver's seat, checking his rearview mirror. The second truck pulled up behind Wilbur, and the red taillights illuminated the cab.

"Holy shit," Murven said. "That's Jesper."

"Shush," Willem said, putting his fingers to his lips and shaking his head.

Wilbur gave Jesper a wave in the mirror and turned right onto the highway. Jesper waved back and followed. As the trucks rolled off into the distance, Willem slid over the roof and back through the window. "Let's go," he said. Murven kicked his legs and swung into his seat.

"What the hell is Jesper doing with Wilbur?" Willem said, steering onto the highway. He and Murven kept silent as they tailed the trucks. Wilbur and Jesper led them deep into the boonies, over the hills and through twists and turns in the narrow country road.

Willem, almost hypnotized by the red lights, mentally compiled the details he'd learned about his brothers. Money laundering. Bank transfers.

Murder. A hot flash rushed over him as he thought about how little he actually knew about his brothers. The tires rumbled over railroad tracks, breaking Willem's trance.

"Turn right up here," Murven said.

Willem drove over more railroad tracks and onto a service road.

"This leads to the train yard," Murven said, bending forward and pointing. "There must be miles of parked train cars along this stretch."

Willem narrowed his eyes as the truck lights flickered off in the distance. He hit the brakes, jolting Murven forward, and slammed the GTO into reverse. He backed the car off the road and over the tracks, maneuvering his way between two train cars and keeping the front end of the car pointed towards the highway. He killed the engine and reached under the seat for the pistol.

"What're you doing?" Murven's eyes darted between Willem and the train yard.

Willem clenched his jaw, pushed the door open and kicked his legs to the ground. He jogged towards the trucks with the pistol in both hands, ready to shoot anything in his way.

"Shit," Murven said. He jumped out of the GTO and scanned the area before sprinting to catch up with

Willem. They crept through the train cars, Willem and his pistol in the lead. The sound of muffled voices grew louder, and Willem spotted flashlight beams and the long shadows of legs extending under the train cars. He held the gun in his right hand, pointed at Murven and then to the ground with his left. Murven gave a thumb's-up and ducked to hide in the train axle.

Willem continued towards the voices, alone. He held the gun in front of him and walked sideways with his back against the train car. He slid to the corner and poked his head around. He watched as Wilbur spoke to a hobo and Jesper supervised two others who were taking cargo from the train and loading it onto the moving trucks. Willem jerked his head back when Jesper looked in his direction. He took a deep breath, unsure if Jesper had seen him. He bit his bottom lip, raised the pistol, and stepped out from behind the train. "You always were a damn crook, Wilbur," he said, as he aimed the gun at Jesper.

Wilbur reached behind his back and put his hand on his pistol. "Willem," he said, glancing at Jesper then back at Willem, "you should be long gone, son."

Jesper drew his gun and fired. Willem dove to the ground as the bullet whizzed past his head and ricocheted off the train car. The hobos dropped the cargo and scattered.

"Jesper! Not yet, dammit!" Wilbur shouted.

"Shut up, Wilbur! His ass is mine," Jesper said, shooting his pistol as he ran towards Willem.

Willem crawled behind the train on his elbows and knees as Jesper's bullets pinged off the ground around him. He balled up behind the wheel, checked himself for gunshot wounds, and dove under the train car. As he lay out flat on the ground, he fired a shot into Jesper's knee.

Jesper fell to the ground and shouted, "You're dead!"

"Willem!" Wilbur shouted from behind the trucks. "You're a bigger dumbass than I thought."

"Why you settin' me up?" Willem hollered. He pushed himself up and squatted behind the train wheel.

"Why'd you kill Mom and Dad?" Wilbur hollered back.

Willem's stomach dropped. The pistol slipped in his hands as he pivoted his shoulders to shout back at Wilbur. He leaned too far over, and a bullet grazed his ear. As he recoiled behind the wheel, blood dripped down the back of his neck. With his back pressed against the train wheel, he looked for Murven but couldn't remember which train car he'd left him behind. Bouncing on his toes, he took a deep breath and adjusted his grip on the pistol.

"One, two, three," he whispered to himself, and stood to make a break for it.

"Now!" Wilbur's voice echoed through the train yard. He and Jesper emptied their guns. Bullets zinged off the train wheels as Willem ducked his head and tucked in his arms.

An engine revved in the distance, and Willem heard the sound of tires chirping towards him between gunshots. As he looked under his elbow, headlights lit up the train yard. The engine roared closer and the tire chirping turned to a screech as Murven hauled ass into the middle of the gunfight, whipping the rear end of the GTO around in a boot-legger spin. Willem popped out from behind the train and bolted for the GTO, shooting out the tires on both moving trucks before diving in the passen-ger-side window. Bullets thumped against the trunk and cracked the rear windshield as Murven gunned it out of the train yard.

Willem twisted in his seat, putting pressure on his injured ear, and looked back. "They ain't comin'," he said.

The GTO wiggled from side to side as Murven steered it down the service road.

"You a'ight?" Murven asked, as he turned onto the highway.

Willem nodded, sat back in his seat, and stared into the rearview mirror at the dark road behind them. As he pressed his hand against his injured ear, he thought about his brothers again. Willard and Walmer were up to God knows what with Commissioner Bristol. Wilton ran a money laundering business with Poot. Wilbur looted trains for a living and was most likely framing him for murder. A family full of crooks. He could get over that. Even being framed for murder didn't compare to what burned him up inside.

Wilbur, and probably the other three, believed he had killed their parents. That he could never get past. Willem rubbed his bloody hand on his jeans as he plotted his next move. Not only did he have to clear his and Murven's name of murder, he had to find the cause of the fire that killed his parents and prove to his brothers once and for all he was not to blame. He looked down at his blood-covered t-shirt, kicked the dashboard and said, "Dang."

## Chapter Fifteen

Willem sat on a plastic stool and leaned against the cabinets under the cigarette display at Roger Rider's Quick Stop. He pressed a wad of paper towels against his bloody ear and watched as Murven and Roger pulled the security camera from the ceiling. Roger, an old high school buddy of Willem and Murven's, owned the gas station and convenience store that was located so far out in the boonies that he rarely saw any customers.

"We're almost ready," Murven said, as he leaned over the counter. "We just gotta figure out how to get sound."

Willem had agreed to let Murven record his own video for the news. He was tired of listening to him rehearse, and after the shootout in the train yard, he didn't care anymore. As his eyes followed Murven racing around the store, his heart rate slowed, the adrenaline began to fade and his wounded right ear throbbed in pain. He tossed the bloodied paper towels on the floor and put two left fingers in the paper towel tube on his lap. He unrolled clean sheets around his right hand and stared at Murven as he replayed the events from the past few days. Wilbur was no angel, but surely not a murderer. He pressed the clean paper towels against his ear and winced at the pain. And Peggy. The pain shot through his jaw. That bullshit about CJ and the fingers. He couldn't think. The pain pulsated in his ear, over his head and down his neck. Willem pushed on his ear with all his strength, fighting back tears and resisting the urge to scream. He bent forward, chest on his knees, and closed his eyes. His thoughts turned to Cindy. He tilted his head up and opened his eyes. Shifting on the stool, he glanced at the phone next to the register. He reached out and picked up the receiver. He had to talk to Cindy to tell her he was safe—for now, at least. He dialed the number with his blood-covered finger.

"Hello," Cindy said after one ring.

"Hey, it's me."

"Where are you? What's wrong?"

"Better if I don't say." Willem's voice raised as pain rushed over his head.

"I can tell you're hurt. What happened?"

"It's really better if I don't say." After the fire, Willem and Cindy had both learned that ignorance was sometimes a blessing. The less Cindy knew the better off they would be if they ended up in a courtroom again. "What's the word?"

"News crews stop by occasionally," Cindy said, "but the deputies keep them away from me. They can't stop Peggy, though."

"Shit. What's she up to?"

"She said her sources told her you're innocent and she can prove it. She said to watch her YouTube channel in the morning."

"What the hell does that mean? You believe her?"

"You know Peggy. Maybe it's true, maybe it's bullshit. Just a sec, hun."

The phone went silent. Willem shifted on the stool and put his head in the corner of the cabinets. He heard the raspy sound of Luna's voice in the background. She was worked up but he couldn't make out what she was saying.

"Holy shit," Cindy said, back on the phone. "Luna said Jesper's callin' in favors to track you down. He's offering five thousand dollars to anybody who finds you."

"Dammit. We better git goin' then. Love ya."

"Shit," Cindy said. "OK. Be safe. I love you."

Willem leaned forward, pushed himself off the stool and hung up the phone. He hunched over in pain, resting his arms on the counter. His entire body ached. "We gotta git, Murven. Now!"

"Y'all need to git the video done first," Roger said, taking the last drag of his cigarette and dropping the butt on the floor. "Tell your side of the story."

Willem, eyeballing Roger, straightened up and walked around the counter to the front door.

"Say a few thangs right quick, Murven." Roger took the camera out of Murven's hand. "We'll git the sound workin'."

"Let's just use one of those little tape recorders for the sound." Murven bounced up on his tiptoes and looked around the store.

Willem stood with his back to the entrance for a moment. Roger had taken more of an interest in the video than he'd expected. Willem pulled the paper towels off his ear as he turned to look out to the parking lot. He spotted Roger's tow truck parked by the road. He rotated in small steps, his ear throbbing with every move, and shuffled towards Roger. "Gotta ditch our ride. Wanna make a trade? GTO for tow truck?" Roger was a drag racing fan and had a reputation for dealing in stolen car parts. Willem figured it would be an easy trade.

Roger checked his phone and looked out the front door. "Gotta test drive her first."

"You're better off not being seen in that thang," Murven said, putting batteries in a tape recorder.

"I'll get the keys for ya after we shoot the video." Roger's eye shifted between Willem and Murven. "You got time." Roger pretended to aim the camera with one hand while he stared at his phone that was clutched in the other.

Willem looked at Murven, who was fidgeting with the tape recorder and mouthing lines, then looked back at Roger. "We need to git outta here. Now!" Willem pressed his ear and swatted the camera out of Roger's hand. "Hurry up and git them keys."

"A'ight." Roger peeked at his phone. "Keys are in the back." He backed away, looking past Willem and out the door, and disappeared into the stock room.

Willem scowled and dropped the wad of paper towels. He grabbed Murven's shoulder and pushed him towards the back exit.

"What the hell, man?" Murven stumbled to keep up.

Roger hopped out of the stock room, cocked his shotgun, and pointed it at Willem's chest. "Sorry," he said with a shrug. "I owe Jesper. Y'all are my ticket to a clean slate."

"You sold us out." Willem stood with the shotgun pressed against his chest, staring into Roger's eyes.

"You were never gonna record my statement were you, asshole?" Murven spit and flipped Roger the bird.

Roger pushed Willem away with the tip of the shotgun and waved him and Murven towards the door with the barrel. As they walked to the entrance at gunpoint, the glass rattled in the door frame and the sound of an engine rumbled in the distance.

"Shit," Willem said when a set of headlights bounced into view. He bit his lip and shook his head, looking back at Roger.

The rumble turned to a roar and floodlights lit up the parking lot. A royal blue 1999 Chevy Silverado monster truck with "The Monster Mesh" painted on the door rolled up in front of the Quick Stop. The 80's heavy metal blasting from the cab stopped mid song, the door swung open and Scott "Squarsh" Washington dropped to the ground. Squarsh, a monster truck driver and amateur dare devil, moonlighted as muscle for Jesper. Next to Jesper himself, he was the worst person who could've arrived.

Squarsh bent over and pulled his stonewashed jeans down over his cowboy boots. His curly mullet, which hung down to the back of his knees, flopped over his face with the motion. As he stood up, he flung his head back and his mullet sliced through the air like a sword. He slammed the truck door shut and pivoted around on the heel of his boot. He twitched his right arm, then his left, adjusting the trademark black mesh tank top he wore year round, regardless of the weather. He gave the others inside the store two thumbs up and a giant grin as he walked towards the entrance.

Squarsh pushed the door open and winked at Roger. "Got 'em all rounded up for me. 'Preciate it."

"You gonna tell Jesper I helped ya, right?" Roger's hands shook and he avoided direct eye contact with Squarsh.

Squarsh ignored Roger and slapped both hands down flat on the store counter. He hopped in the air and swung his feet over the countertop. After sizing up the store, he reached up and took a can of Skoal from the dispenser over the cash register, then stared at Willem as he packed his dip. "Did you really shoot Jesper in the knee?" Squarsh said.

Willem tilted his head. "Did I?"

"You're one crazy son of a gun, boy, I'll tell ya what. And Murven." Murven stood up straight. Squarsh wagged his finger and said, "This is how you treat family?"

Murven looked Squarsh in the eye. "Jesper

changed."

"Well, you two are in deep shit." Squarsh walked around the counter, putting the can of dip in his back pocket. "Jesper wants you dead, Willem. I'm not sure about you, Murven."

Willem looked over at Roger, who still clutched the shotgun in his shaking hand. "You really wanna do this? Get me killed?"

"Sorry," Roger said, his voice cracking. "I done called Jesper. He knows you're here. I didn't know he was gonna kill ya." Roger lowered the shotgun, his eyes darting between Willem and Squarsh. With trembling hands, Roger reached for his pack of smokes in his shirt pocket. But he was unable to stop shaking; he gave up on the smokes and took a step back. With a gulp, he raised his weapon at Squarsh.

Squarsh swung his right arm under the shotgun and kicked his right leg around in a circle. As he twirled, he snatched the shotgun out of Roger's hand, his mullet swishing like a whip, snapping across Roger's face. Squarsh completed his spin and said, "Hurts like hell, don't it?" He chuckled as Roger rubbed the lash marks on his cheek. Squarsh rested the shotgun on his shoulder and smiled at Willem and Murven. "Get in the back of the truck."

Willem and Murven walked side by side out the door. Willem pressed his ear and looked back at

Squarsh, who had shotgun in one hand and Roger's neck in the other. "Don't even think about running," Squarsh said.

At the rear of the truck, Willem waited for Murven to pull himself over the tailgate. Once Murven's feet dropped out of sight, Willem put his foot on the bumper, let go of his ear and hoisted himself up and over into the bed of the truck. As he pushed himself towards the cab with his legs, he heard Squarsh say, "Tape 'em up. Arms and legs."

Roger flopped over the tailgate, coughing and out of breath, with a roll of duct tape in his hand. "Sorry," Roger said, as he picked at the end of the tape.

"You're an asshole," Murven said.

Squarsh peered over the bed of the truck and waved the shotgun over his head. "Shut the hell up."

Roger taped Willem's wrists behind his back and wrapped his ankles tight. He did the same to Murven, then climbed out of the truck.

Willem squinted his eyes in pain and stared at Murven, shifting on his side, looking for a comfortable position. The truck door slammed and the engine revved. Willem cringed as heavy metal screamed from the speakers. The floodlights flickered off the road signs, and he and Murven bounced like popcorn as the truck thundered onto the highway.

"Hey," Murven said over the noise. "I got a knife in my back pocket."

Willem and Murven rolled over and scooted back to back. Struggling to stay in one place, Willem felt for Murven's pocket knife with his bound hands. He squeezed the knife between two fingers and scooped it into his palm. After pushing away from Murven, Willem popped the pocket knife open and cut through his own tape. Keeping flat, he climbed around Murven and slashed through the duct tape on his wrists and ankles. He fought to maintain balance on all fours and poked his head up to look through the tinted rear window of the cab, unable to see inside. Willem flipped over onto his butt and folded the knife closed. "We gotta jump."

Murven peeked over the side of the truck, then slid down, bracing himself with both hands. He locked eyes with Willem and nodded.

The engine quieted and the truck coasted through a wide left turn. "Jump into the kudzu. Go!" Willem kicked Murven's leg. Murven stepped his foot up on the passenger side edge of the truck bed and pushed off. Willem crawled under the cab window and wriggled up to a squat. In one motion, he thrust himself up and out of the truck. As the kudzu leaves slapped his face, he tucked his knees and hollered, "Dang!"

# Chapter Sixteen

Peggy balanced on a chair and stretched her hands over her head. She held one corner of the blue tarp against the ceiling, positioning the staple gun and then squeezing the trigger, shooting the staple into the ceiling with a hollow thud. She pivoted, running the tarp through her fingers, stretching and stapling the second corner with the same thump. Her newsroom was coming together. She had plans to convert her kitchen eventually, but that dumbass CJ had caused her to move up her timetable. He'd screwed it all up from the get-go. The more she improvised, the more CJ unwittingly torpedoed her efforts. Now he'd gotten to her sources and almost destroyed her plans for her big investigative journalist exposé, uncovering countywide corruption—topped off by cracking the murder case.

She hopped down from the chair, sticking the landing, and spread out her cue cards on the table. She fidgeted with her teeth, then put her fingertips on the cards and slid them around on the table, considering the best order for presentation. Start with Willem and Murven. Move on to the other Wisely brothers. Mention Poot and Terry. That made the most sense. That damn CJ was last. She'd sting his ass good and finish with a strong hook to draw in the viewers for the final report.

Holding her hands on her chest, she thought about losing her tape from the commissioner's office as she walked around to the other side of the table. Her heart pounded. That damn CJ. She flipped the clamps on the legs of her tripod so hard they nearly broke off. She took a deep breath. She couldn't report angry. She positioned the tripod and placed the camera on top. CJ ruined everything. The anger swelled up inside of her and she slapped the table top with both hands, bouncing the cue cards. Control, she told herself. Her report would fix CJ. The thought of revenge eased her nerves.

She straightened the cords dangling from the camera and plugged them into her TV. The events of the last couple days had pushed her to the limit. She had to adapt. She was getting good at that. Her body tingled as excitement and frustration pulsed through her veins. CJ ruined her plan but she had everything she needed to make him regret it.

She picked up the camera's remote control and circled back around to her news desk. She pulled the wrinkles out of the tarp and sat down in front of it, facing the camera. She looked at her image on the TV screen, turning her head from side to side and sliding the chair to find the perfect position. She looked pretty good on TV. She was sure to get noticed after this report. She brushed her hair, using her image on the TV as a mirror, and ran through the order one last time. Willem and Murven. Wisely boys. Poot. Terry. That dumbass CJ. Then the hook.

She smiled wide to loosen her face muscles, adjusted her teeth and rested her hands on the table. With a glance at the TV, she pressed record on the camera remote. After waiting a few seconds—she had learned to leave some space at the beginning for editing—she looked into the camera. "Hello and welcome. I'm Peggy Vanderbilt and you're watching 'Peggy.'" Peggy bounced her eyebrows and stacked her papers like the news anchors do on the six o'clock news.

"As I'm sure y'all know, the last few days have been quite eventful. Willem Wisely has been accused of murder and is running from the law with his allegedly accomplice Murven Holliday.

But I'm here to tell ya Willem and Murven are not the killers." Peggy leaned into the camera and grinned. "I know who the killer is and I can prove it."

She pressed pause on the remote, ran around the table and moved the camera to the left to adjust the angle. Camera number two. She ran back to her seat, sat down facing the camera one position and adjusted her teeth. She pressed record then turned to camera two. "But first let me set the scene for y'all. We all know Willem just barely avoided being convicted of murder a while ago. His dad and mama died in a horrible house fire. He was accused of setting it but I never believed he did it. Willem Wisely is not capable of murder. And Murven Holliday? Well, that boy's too lazy for murder. Killing takes a certain amount of effort. In all my years I ain't never seen Murven Holliday put effort into anything but being stupid. I'm sure if you know Murven you'll agree. But Willem's brothers—" Peggy jumped up and pressed pause in one move. She repositioned the camera, ran around the table and sat down. She hit record and turned to camera number three. "They ain't so innocent."

Peggy looked into the camera with a blank stare. "I'm gonna expose some people, some of them friends, because it's the right thang to do. I might be crucified for this, but I don't care. I'm a journalist. My loyalty is to the truth."

Peggy pressed pause and inhaled through her nose. Adrenaline made her giddy. She chuckled once, just to get it out of her system and pressed record. "Let me start with those Wisely boys. Every one of 'em, not including Willem, of course, is into somethin' no good. Take Wilton Wisely. Him and Pete Barber are running a money laundering business. Yep. That's right. Haven't you ever wondered why it's so easy not to pay Poot rent?" Peggy looked into the camera, turned her head to the side and raised her left eyebrow.

"And how 'bout those two older Wiselys. Willard and Walmer. They seem like perfect goody two shoes, with high payin' corporate-type jobs in the big city. But that's all a bunch'a hogwash. They're up to something behind the scenes. They got somethin' going with our own Chief County Commissioner Terry Bristol. Y'all may not believe me but I can prove it. Everything I'm telling you today I can prove." Peggy stacked her cue cards, slapped them on the table and crossed her arms, letting the camera run for dramatic effect.

"And now for the worst of the Wiselys." She shook her head and leaned forward. "Wilbur. That boy ain't never done nothin' good, and he's more than willing to let his own baby brother take the fall for his crimes. He's a train robbin', cigarette smuggling crook. That I can prove, too."

Peggy pressed pause and closed her eyes. She inhaled, opened her eyes and hit record. "And last but not least. The county crybaby and extortioner, Deputy CJ Maddocks. How many of y'all are feedin' him tidbits? Does his daddy know about his games? Ole CJ is into much more than forcing information. If you see that little turd all you gotta do is say 'Hey, CJ! How 'bout them fingers.' That'll git his goat good. Soon you'll never have to feed his ass another damn tidbit again. I guarantee ya." Peggy's face twitched and her hands shook. She pressed pause and raised her arms over her head. That damn CJ. She lowered her arms. Almost finished.

She forced a fake smile, pressed record and looked into the camera. "Like I said, I can prove every single thang I said here today. I got proof. I've been doing extensive research with the help of my research assistant Handy Drucker." Peggy's real smile returned. "I'll show you all of my proof and reveal the identity of the killer on the next episode of 'Peggy.' Be sure to tune in!"

Peggy pressed stop and squeezed her fists. She loved the adrenaline, and she sure as hell screwed that damn CJ. The rush rejuvenated her aging body.

She slid away from the kitchen table, disconnected the camera and danced her way to her computer. After connecting her camera and starting the upload to her computer, she pushed her curtains aside and peeked out the window. Almost sunrise. She had to get moving.

She danced into the kitchen and opened the fridge. Fried chicken and mashed potatoes with gravy—her signature dish every year at the county cookout—sat on the center shelf on top of days' worth of leftovers. She kicked the fridge closed, holding the paper plate over her head with one hand and popping the microwave open with the other. As she watched the plate spin, she commended herself on remembering all the lies she'd told. Then a hint of remorse crept in. Willem didn't deserve to take the fall. The bell dinged and she shook it off. She pinched the sides of the hot plate, and after pulling it in close for a whiff, sat it on the counter. She bent down and grabbed an old salt shaker with duct tape over the holes from under the sink. She peeled the tape away from her special seasoning—an Internet recipe—and dashed just the right amount over the chicken and mashed potatoes before covering the plate with aluminum foil.

With a leap and a whirl, she sat the plate by the door and pranced to her computer. After settling into her desk chair, she slipped her teeth in and out and watched herself on the screen. Not bad for a mature lady. She clipped the first few seconds of the video, spliced in her prerecorded introduction and credits, and exported her video to YouTube. She'd done this so many times she could do it in her sleep. While the video loaded, she reclined in her chair and daydreamed about the accolades and job offers she'd receive after this report. When the video was online, she clicked play and slid her phone out of the leg pocket of her camouflage cargo pants. As she watched the final version, she scrolled through her contact list and called Sheriff Happy's home number.

"What?" the sheriff said.

"Hey, Sheriff, It's me."

"Dammit, Peggy. I'm trying to sleep."

"Yeah, well, you best watch my YouTube channel right now 'cause you're damn sure gonna hear about it." Peggy hung up the phone and laughed. No doubt the sheriff would watch.

She looked at the clock on the wall. Time to hit the road. Her equipment, which she'd laid out on the couch next to her oversized purse, was prepped and set to go. She held her purse open with one hand and packed with the other, mentally checking off her supply list. Satisfied she had all her gear and back-up provisions, she put on her camo jacket and thrust the bag straps over her shoulder. Supporting her purse with her hip, she leaned over her computer and refreshed her video page. Ten hits already. Peggy scooped up the plate of chicken and nudged the trailer door open with her foot. She took one last look at her computer screen before leaving and said, "Dang."

# Chapter Seventeen

Deputy CJ swiveled back and forth in his desk chair, wiping the sweat off his forehead with the back of his hand, and waited for Deputy John Gordy, the only other person in the office, to leave. Willem knew about the fingers. CJ's hands shook and his stomach fluttered. Willem couldn't possibly know about the fire, too. CJ needed time alone in the office to retrace his tracks. He must have let something slip. He bounced his legs and rubbed his sweaty palms on his knees. His eyes followed Deputy Gordy walking to the sign-out board.

"Later, CJ," Gordy said, picking up his bag.

"Later." CJ heard the anxiety in his own voice.

The door closed and CJ floundered to his feet. He hustled to the file cabinet and jerked the "W" drawer open, pulling it off the tracks. He scooped his hand under all the files, tucked them in his arms and lugged them to his desk. He flipped through the files and tossed them into stacks, separating the Wisely files from the others while leaving sweaty finger-prints on the folders. One pile for Willem. One for Wilbur. One for the fire. The other three brothers had no official police records. Anything not Wisely-related, he chucked on the floor.

He locked his fingers behind his neck and shifted his eyes from file to file. It all started with the fire. Make sure the fire case was airtight then move on to the murders. He dried his hands on his shirt and picked up the file labeled "Wisely Fire." He skimmed the first page to refresh his memory, holding the file away from his face to avoid drops of sweat. He was the first to respond to the fire. He wrote all the reports. He transcribed the written documents to the computer files. He controlled all the information. He checked signatures, verified the chain of evidence and read the court transcript, confirming his testi-mony matched the evidence report. He clapped the folder closed and exhaled. Nothing to worry about.

CJ unbuttoned his shirt and fanned his face with the file. Everything in the report was all technically true. The fire marshal really did say the fire was started with gasoline and that it was most likely arson. All he did was tweak the evidence to make it look like Willem was the culprit. His chest tightened as he thought about ways he may have messed up. But no. He made it through the trial without getting caught. No one questioned the reports or the evidence.

As the sweat evaporated and cooled his face, he relaxed and remembered the beauty of his plan. The fire had come at the perfect time. He'd just gotten serious about writing his first novel, and he was gaining traction with his tidbit scheme. The fire was the perfect case for him to exploit and not piss off a bunch of bad-ass crooks. It had all the ingredients he needed. Tragic death. Mysterious arson. And a patsy with probable motive who wasn't likely to fight back. Willem was a good guy. Low key and direct, but not all that determined. Everybody in the county had heard rumors that he and Cindy were having money problems. He was an easy target. Hide a few gas cans. Omit a few details. Embellish a couple others and the next thing CJ knew, Willem was on trial for murder.

The plan was good but he'd leveraged it all wrong. The trial went faster than he'd anticipated; Willem got off due to lack of physical evidence, and the story never built enough momentum to make it beyond a brief mention in statewide headlines. His own efforts to boost the story failed. His articles were labeled biased and fabricated, leading to his dismissal from the newspaper. CJ swore the next time he framed somebody he'd be damn sure to plant plenty of physical evidence to get a conviction, or at least enough to keep the trial going longer, and he would focus his reporting mostly on the facts.

CJ sank down into his desk chair, lost in recollection. He reclined for a moment then flailed to his feet. The fingers. The murders. The teeth. He slapped his hands on his face and squeezed his cheeks as he bounced on his knees, unsure what to do next. As he gazed down at the files on his desk, deliberating his next move, his cell phone rang. He checked the caller ID and said, "Hey, Deddy."

"Peggy called. Watch her YouTube channel. Now! I'm coming in. Keep your ass in that office!"

CJ's hand trembled as he clicked to Peggy's channel. He stood behind his desk, watching and sweating as Peggy reported. He chewed his fingernails, biting the tip of his thumb, when she mentioned Poot and Terry. Wide-eyed, he stopped breathing when she said, "Hey, CJ! How 'bout them fingers." When the report finished, he collapsed into his chair and ran his fingers through his oily hair. It was Peggy. She told Willem about the fingers. Peggy knew everything. The fingers. The teeth. The bodies. Peggy could expose his whole scheme.

CJ sat frozen, staring at the floor. Waves of anxiety prickled across his body. He dumped the trash can, put it between his feet and flopped his head down on the desk. As he fought the urge to puke, the office phone rang. He snatched the receiver and held it against his oily-wet ear. "Sheriff's office."

"Well, hey there, sugar. You watch 'Peggy' this morning?"

"You old harpy!" CJ kicked the trash can and jumped to his feet. "You're fulla shit! Your name ain't even Vanderbilt!"

"My stage name ain't none of your damn business, hun"

"You ain't got no evidence against me, you crazy hag!"

"I got all the proof I need. I even got one of those hobo teeth you tried to file down to look like a vampar tooth."

"What?" CJ paused. "I didn't file no damn teeth. Why the hell would I do that?"

"To git them vampars in your story, dumbass."

"That don't make no kinda sense. Vampires don't lose teeth."

"Well, that's what I'm reporting. Everybody will

believe me anyways, once I show them my other evidence."

"You're evidence is fake as your teeth!"

"It's real enough, sugar. I know about more than just the dead hobos, too. I know all your tidbits. Enough to send you away for a long time. And with the new evidence that's gonna appear today, you're done."

"Uh, uh." CJ muttered, unable to speak.

"This is my story you little shit and I'm not letting you steal it from me. I'll kill you if I have to."

CJ pulled the phone away from his ear. "You're crazy!"

"Have fun in prison." Peggy's tone changed. "Thanks for making me famous." The line went dead.

CJ sat down with a gasp and rocked in his chair, pulling his hair and mumbling. If Peggy knew all his tidbits, he really was in some deep shit. His chest tightened. Peggy bugged the commissioner's office. She must have bugged his office, too. He laid back in his chair, tucked in his knees and kicked his desk away from the wall with both feet, falling backwards to the floor. He rolled to his elbows and knees, followed the phone cords to the wall, and studied the wall jack. It looked undisturbed. He pushed himself up on his knees, his sweaty palms sliding on the floor.

That old crone Peggy had gained access to some serious information. Somewhere he'd let something slip. His chest contracted and he gulped in air. His daddy's office. He twitched as a bead of sweat ran down his neck. Sometimes he sat in his daddy's chair when he was alone. He liked to extort tidbits from that phone. He bounded to his feet and raced to the sheriff's office. With a side kick, he crashed through the door, ripping it out of the frame, and stumbled into the office. "How does she know!" he hollered, as he lowered his shoulder and rammed the desk. He dove to the floor and scrambled to find the phone jack. As he fed the cord through his fingers he heard the front door open.

"Junior!" the sheriff shouted.

CJ's skin grew hot and the sweat covering his body turned ice cold. On all fours, he walked his head around to look out the office door. The floor pounded, vibrating through his fingers with each of his daddy's approaching footsteps.

"What the hell are you doing?" Sheriff Happy kicked the door across the room.

"It's Peggy, Deddy," CJ whined from the floor, "I think she's got the office bugged."

"What?"

"She bugged Terry Bristol's office. I caught her

climbing out of his window." CJ sat back on his knees and straightened his back. "I got the tape."

The sheriff snatched CJ's collar and heaved him to his feet. "Git the tape," he said, shaking the sweat off his hand that he'd wrung out of CJ's shirt.

CJ scurried to his desk and fumbled the top drawer open. He pushed pens and paperclips aside and placed his hand on the tape.

"What's all that bullshit Peggy said about the fingers?" Sheriff Happy walked towards the deputy, looking around the office.

CJ kept his head down and pretended to feel around for the tape. "I don't know, Deddy. I thank she's tryin' to frame me for the murders."

"You tidbitin' with this murder case, boy?" the sheriff said in a low voice.

CJ scrunched his eyebrows as he took the tape out of the drawer. He was never sure if his daddy knew about the tidbits or not. He always figured it was best not to ask. He held the tape up to the sheriff, shaking his head from side to side. "No, sir, Deddy."

"I'll listen in the car." Sheriff Happy snatched the tape out of his son's hand. "I'm going to bring in Handy. Keep your ass in this office. Don't leave for anything. And no more tidbitin'!"

CJ saluted as the door slammed. He looked around the office at the scattered papers and the splintered door frame leading to his daddy's office. He pulled his sweat-drenched shirt away from his chest and said, "Dang."

# Chapter Eighteen

Willem lumbered through the underbrush, looking up through the trees at the pink sunrise. He and Murven had zigzagged through the woods for hours, staying clear of the roads. The getaway left him with a few more scratches and bruises, but none of that mattered. His bullet-grazed ear hurt like hell and obscured any of the other pain. Out of breath, he put his hands on his knees and collapsed onto a moss-covered boulder. "Stop," he shouted.

"You a'ight?" Murven said, bouncing down the hill and showing no signs of distress. Murven could leap from anything, moving or not, and walk away unscathed.

"Yep." Willem spit and laid back flat on the boulder. "Peggy's up to sumpin'."

"What do you mean?" Murven sat down next to him.

"She knows shit. She knows sumpin' about CJ and the fingers. She knows about Wilbur."

"We need to talk to Peggy, then." Murven reclined and stared at the sky.

Willem propped himself up on his elbows. "She ain't gonna tell us jack shit. We need to talk to Handy. He's bound to know sumpin'."

"Long as he don't lock us up again." Murven rolled off the side of the boulder and on to his feet. "Mars Diner ain't far." Mars diner was a popular breakfast spot with the locals, and they knew most of the regulars. They could borrow, or if necessary steal, a car from somebody.

Murven led the way. Willem walked a few paces behind, keeping an eye on the way they'd come. When the diner came into view through the trees, Willem jogged to catch up with Murven. They hid in the woods along the backside of the parking lot and watched as the breakfast crowd drifted in.

"That's Tinker." Murven pointed to a rusted out '85 Pontiac Grand Am rattling into the parking lot. Tinker Taylor parked by the dumpster and took his time unwedging himself from between the seat and the steering wheel. Once out of the car, he pulled his pants up over his butt crack and limped towards the diner.

"Psst. Tinker." Murven shook the tree branch. "Over here."

Tinker stopped, and after catching his breath, turned around. He crouched down and looked through the trees. "Well, I'll be. That you, Murven? Willem with ya?" Tinker glanced back at the diner, pulling his pants up under his beer belly, and wobbled to the tree line.

"Yeah. Git over here." Murven drifted back into the trees.

"Holy sheep shit. What the hell happened to y'all."

"Too much to say," Willem said, checking for any onlookers in the diner. "Peggy post a video?"

"You damn skippy she did. She said some shit about Poot, Terry and your brothers. 'Parently she can prove y'all are innocent, too."

"She say how?" Willem asked.

Tinker shook his head. "Nah, she just said to tune in next time."

"We need a car," Willem said. "Can you help us out?"

Tinker scratched his belly with both hands and spit. "I reckon. Gives me a reason to be late for work. Just don't ding it up none." Tinker unclipped his keys from his belt and tossed them to Murven. "And if y'all git caught, I'm sayin' ya stole it."

Murven gave Tinker a pat on the shoulder and jogged to the car.

"'Preciate it," Willem said, as he ran past Tinker. He hopped in the passenger side and sank down into the seat. "I need to sleep." Willem closed his eyes, and despite his aching body, he drifted off to sleep. He woke to Murven slapping his shoulder.

"Wake up! We're here!" Murven shouted.

Willem blinked his eyes, struggling to wake up, and looked out the window as they were passing the Rose Blossom sign.

"Damn, I thought you were dead, son." Murven gave Willem one last slap on the shoulder.

Willem stretched and squirmed himself upright, squinting to see as the morning sun beamed through the windshield. He tapped his ear. The pain had eased. "Truck's here. Handy must still be hidin'."

"No tellin'," Murven said, as he parked next to the garbage truck and killed the engine.

Willem got out and hooked his arms over the door. "Handy! Handy!" he hollered.

"Y'all here to whoop my ass?" Handy's voice reverberated through the trailer park.

"Where are you?" Willem shouted, looking around. "We need information."

"You gonna lock us in your bunker again?" Murven said.

Willem waved his hand and shook his head at Murven. "Don't scare him off."

Static crackled through the speakers mounted on the tops of the trailers closest to the gate. "I'm sorry I locked y'all up. I read my evidence wrong. There ain't no nexus and y'all ain't martyrs. I think I'm supposed to be helping y'all. I can see the signs clear now."

"Martyrs?" Murven said. He blocked the sun with his hand and moved towards the speakers. The static cut off and he stopped in his tracks, turning his head to the side to listen. He ran to the gate and looked down the road. "Shit! It's the sheriff!"

Two squad cars pulled up to the gate, lights flashing and sirens blasting.

Willem and Murven hauled ass towards the landfill. Handy popped up on top of the bunker. "This way!" he shouted, waving them to the backside of the half-buried trailer.

Sheriff Happy gunned it through the gate, slamming on the brakes and skidding to a stop just before sliding into the dried-up creek. The sheriff exploded out of the squad car, jumped the creek and high-stepped across the trailer park, mustering the speed he was known for in his high school football days.

Three deputies fanned out from the vehicles and joined the pursuit.

As Willem and Murven cut around the bunker, Murven turned back and hollered, "You call the news yet?"

Willem grabbed Murven's shirt and yanked him around the trailer. He looked back to see the sheriff closing in fast.

When they reached the backside of the bunker, they spotted Handy standing by the chain-link fence. Without hesitation, they sprinted towards him.

"Roll! Roll! Roll!" Handy swung his arm and held up the bottom of the fence.

Willem slid on his leg, laid out flat, and rolled under the fence. He sprang to his feet and snatched up the bottom of the fence as Murven tumbled past.

Handy dropped on his side and rolled under. Kicking his feet over his head, he backwards somersaulted to his feet. "Through the maze!" he said, adjusting his glasses. He led them downhill to the entrance. "Try to keep up."

Handy shot through the maze like a chubby lab rat. Willem scrambled behind him, looking back at each twist and turn to keep from losing Murven. The high walls of the maze were made of sheet metal and appliances, all stacked flush and just wide enough for one person. Handy stopped in a large corridor and pointed down one of three paths. "Right, left, left, right." He pushed his glasses up on his nose. "Got it?"

"What?" Willem said, as Murven bumped into him from behind.

"I'm breaking off for recon. Follow this path. Right, left, left, right at the intersections. I'll catch up." Handy opened a refrigerator door in the wall of the maze and disappeared through it.

Willem glanced back at Murven before leading the way down the narrowest of the three passages. The dirt under his feet sloped downwards, and sections of the maze were covered overhead. Willem took the first right, the first left and ran his left hand along the wall, searching for the next turn. He reached the end of the passage and stepped out into a circular corridor. His eyes tracked along the curved walls. "Shit," he said, "Which one's left?"

"Where did we come from?" Murven said, spinning around.

A dented dryer door in the wall popped open behind Willem. Handy scooted out feet first and lowered himself to the ground. "You missed the turn. Follow me."

Willem and Murven fell in behind Handy and backtracked through the maze. They turned twice before Handy stopped and pulled open the door to an industrial freezer. "Head towards that speck of light."

"Wait," Willem said. "Why are you helping us? This a trick?"

"I told you," Handy said, pushing up his glasses. "I was wrong before. The evidence told me I'm supposed to help. Sorry 'bout last time and shit."

Shaking his head, Willem pushed Murven through first and stepped sideways into the narrow passage. The door slammed behind him, the speck of light the only thing visible. If Handy wanted to trap them again he'd succeeded. They squeezed their way down the tight tunnel, and the stench of mildew grew stronger.

"Holy shit," Murven said, stretching his arms and rotating his shoulders. The tunnel fed into a room that was lit by beams of sunlight shining through air shafts in the ceiling.

"Hot damn." Willem stood at the entrance, waving his hand in front of his nose.

Murven ran across the dry-rotted Persian rug and flopped down on the tattered couch along the back wall. "This is nicer than my trailer."

"What the hell is this place?" Willem pushed on the wall, testing the stability.

"Safe room!" Handy said, appearing out of nowhere.

"Holy shit!" Murven jumped and hit his head on the ceiling.

"Sheriff ain't even following the maze," Handy said. "He's just tryin' to kick through shit. That ain't gonna work." Handy tapped his knuckles on the metal wall and opened a functioning fridge. "Y'all got time. Want sumpin' to drink?"

Murven glanced at Willem and sat up to peak in the fridge. "I'll take a Coke."

Handy passed Murven a can of Coke and cracked one open for himself.

"You really are helping us," Willem said.

Handy looked up at Willem over the top of his glasses, reminding him again of the chubby outcast he knew in high school. "Tell us what you know about Peggy," Willem said.

""Not shit." Handy sipped his drink. "I can't find a damn thang on her. And I've tried. Believe me."

Willem scratched his head and lowered his arm, rubbing his finger over his ear. "What about CJ?"

"Not much on him, either. He burns all the paper from the sheriff's office."

"Burns the paper?" Willem raised his chin and looked down at Handy. "Where?"

"Behind the sheriff's office, mostly. Sometimes he does it at his writing shed."

"Writing shed?" Murven said.

"He's got a writing shed out in the woods behind the old textile mill. It's sittin' on the creek. Damn thing's about to wash away."

"What does he do in a writin' shed?" Willem asked.

"Writes. He's got a desk and a chair in there."

"Who else knows about this?" Willem said.

"I told Peggy a while back." Handy sat up straight. "When all this news about the murders broke the other day, she told me to stay away from the place for good."

"Why?" Murven said.

Handy shrugged and sipped his Coke.

"You stay away?" Willem asked.

"Hell, no," Handy said with a snort. "I went out there yesterday and didn't see nothin'. I was gonna go today, too, but probably not now since we're hidin' and shit."

"I wanna see this place. Take us," Willem said, standing over Handy.

Handy sat his Coke on the end table and hoisted himself to his feet. "I'm stayin' here for now." He stepped sideways past Willem. "Y'all can go. Just follow the trail to the creek behind the mill. You'll see the shed."

Willem walked to the passage leading back the

way they'd come. "How the hell do we git outta this place?"

Handy opened a mini-fridge door on the wall next to the functioning fridge and tossed Willem a flashlight. "Slide through here. There's an escape vehicle at the bottom."

Willem flicked on the flashlight and shined it into the escape tunnel. He glanced back at Murven, then raised his eyebrows at Handy.

"It's soft at the bottom." Handy shoved Willem towards the tunnel. "Helmets are on the wall. Follow the tunnel. It'll spit you out on the backside of the landfill."

Willem kicked his legs inside the air duct and scooted his hips forward. Holding the flashlight, he crossed his arms over his chest and dropped into the pitch black shaft. His stomach fluttered and his body tingled as he plunged downward. The air duct curved at the bottom, shooting him out onto cushioning. He tumbled onto his belly and flipped on the flashlight.

"Yee haw!" Murven's muffled scream echoed out of the air duct. Willem scrambled out of the way as Murven bounced onto the mattresses. "That was fun as hell, man," Murven said, rolling over and bouncing.

Willem shined the light across the small room

and gave Murven a quick smile. "Check out that bad boy." He flashed the light over a scrapped-together 4-wheel ATV. "Looks like Handy really is handy."

Murven squeezed the brake lever and slapped the seat. "This'll work."

Willem handed Murven a helmet and looked down the only passageway out of the room.

Murven swung his leg over the seat, grabbed the handlebars and started the ATV. The engine purred. "Not half bad," he said, bobbing his head.

Willem stretched the helmet, keeping it away from his ear as he put it over his head, and climbed on behind Murven.

"You set?" Murven said over his shoulder.

Willem knocked on Murven's helmet. "Let's git."

Murven twisted the throttle, the front wheels bounced off the floor and the ATV fired down the tunnel. Willem held on tight, hoping to hell Murven could see well enough to drive. The ride didn't last long. The tunnel dipped down and curved up. Strips of plastic slapped Willem's helmet as the ATV launched into the air. Willem closed his eyes, blinded by the sunlight, and hugged Murven's waist. The ATV slammed to the ground and the back end fish tailed as Murven steered away from the highway.

"Deputy!" he hollered, hauling ass into the woods.

Willem looked back to the highway. A squad car sat parked at the edge of the landfill but didn't move. "We're good," he shouted.

Murven gave a thumbs up and laid into the throttle.

Willem adjusted his helmet and said, "Dang."

# Chapter Nineteen

CJ chugged a glass of water while reclining in his desk chair and listening to his radio. His daddy and the other deputies had Willem and Murven pinned down at the landfill, which bought him plenty of time to finish covering his tracks. He sat up straight and put his empty glass down between the two stacks of files on his desk.

"Shit," he said under his breath when the phone rang. He tapped his fingers on the desk. The phone had been ringing off the hook for the last hour. He had to answer it. Could be official. Rubbing his queasy stomach, he answered the phone. "Sheriff's office."

"Hey, CJ! How 'bout the fingers!"

CJ slammed the receiver down. The murders should have stimulated his dwindling tidbit scheme, with his snitches pointing fingers at each other and begging him for his protection, but instead they were turning on him. Now, thanks to Peggy's report, he'd been stripped of even the tiniest morsel of control. Nothing had turned out the way he'd expected. His inside knowledge of the murders failed to rejuvenate his journalism career. Not one person mentioned his story to him. Not even the newspaper editor. Peggy got the scoop on him with her stupid bugs. She was toying with him. The knot in his stomach tightened. Peggy said new evidence would "appear." He had a nauseating gut feeling that he knew what she meant. He slapped his cheeks and scooted close to his desk. No time to waste.

CJ licked his finger and thumbed through the smaller stack of reports—his first drafts—that were full of seeds he'd planted to steer the evidence. He knew from Peggy's tape that the seed he'd planted about possible bank transactions between Willem and his brothers had sprouted and grown. He knew first hand that the other seeds had taken root, too. He shook open a plastic grocery bag and chucked in the old reports. He tied the handles in a knot, tossing the bag on the floor. They'd served their purpose.

He picked up the revised versions of the official documents and skimmed each page. His first drafts were good but needed a punch up. The tweaks to the latest versions ensured his own ass was covered and prevented Terry Bristol from doing any of his own tweaking to point the finger at Poot. That prick Terry only cared about cleaning up the county for his image in the upcoming governor's race. CJ sure as hell wouldn't do anything to help Terry. CJ liked Poot better anyway and didn't give a shit how many trailer parks Poot built.

Satisfied with his rewrites, CJ returned the new reports to the file cabinet and pounded the drawer closed with the side of his fist. He put on his cowboy hat and took a last look around the office. As he picked up the grocery bag on the floor, the phone rang. He put his hand on the receiver, then pulled it away. No time for any more bullshit. He had to deal with his squad car. Chester wasn't likely to make a connection between the smell and the fingers but CJ couldn't risk it. He stepped outside and locked the office door.

Tom Riley, a county clerk who was walking into the building next door, shouted, "Hey, CJ! How 'bout them fingers?"

CJ tucked the plastic bag under his arm and waved him off. It was later in the morning than he realized and the town was coming alive. As he passed the diner, he looked in out of habit.

Ray Carson lowered his newspaper and tapped on the window. "Hey, CJ! How 'bout them fingers?"

CJ put his head down and walked sideways with his back to the window. He continued down the street with his cowboy hat over his face. Out of the corner of his eye, he spotted Jack Dawson in front of the hardware store.

Jack stopped sweeping and shouted, "Hey, CJ! How 'bout them fingers!"

CJ flipped him off and kept his eyes to the ground the rest of the way. He made it to Chester's garage without anymore taunts and ducked behind a car parked on the street to scope out the scene. Chester was sitting in his usual place, reading the same damn magazine. CJ scooted along the side of the car and ran on his tiptoes to the back of the garage. He peeked in the window. The garage was empty and Chester hadn't done shit to the squad cars. CJ jiggled the handle to the back door but no luck. Scanning the ground, he spotted a broken car antenna. He forced the wire antenna under the window pane and cracked the glass. He scratched at the cracks with the antenna and picked the shards out of the pane with his fingers. After a pause to slow his heavy breathing, he reached his arm in and unlocked the window. The window rattled open and CJ stuck his head through. Adjusting his cowboy hat, he listened, ready to retreat should Chester come through the door, but nothing happened.

CJ slid through the window and onto the workbench. With his jaw hanging open, he thrust his hips forward and landed with bent knees on the concrete floor. His heart was racing. He crept over to the back of his squad car and pushed on the trunk. The lid creaked open and the stench of the fingers drifted past. He wrinkled his nose and turned away, looking for something to cover the smell. His eyes honed in on the degreaser. Covering his face with his cowboy hat, he sprayed the trunk and listened for Chester over the hiss of the aerosol can. As the degreaser sputtered out, he heard the door to the reception area squeak open. He dropped the can and his hat and turned to face Chester, who was standing in the doorway.

"What the hell are you doin, CJ?" Chester saw the glass on the bench. "You break my window?" He took off his belt, folded it and snapped it together. "Git your ass over here, boy. I'm fixin' to tan your hide."

CJ ran behind his squad car. "Stop, Chester! You can't give me no whoopin'!"

"Like hell I can't. Your daddy done gave me permission to whoop your ass whenever I see fit."

"That was when I was a kid, you dumb old fart!"

Chester snapped his belt and bounced from side to side, trying to corner CJ.

"Gimme the keys to your tow truck." CJ put the bag handles on his wrist and hopped sideways with both hands on the squad car. "Deddy called me for back up."

"Bullshit."

"Dammit, Chester." CJ backed away from the squad car and drew his gun. "Gimme the damn keys."

Chester pointed to some keys that were hanging on the wall by the door. "Dumbass," he said, lowering his belt.

CJ grabbed the keys and flicked his gun towards the storage closet. "You're obstructing an officer. I'm gonna detain you for your own safety."

Chester walked towards CJ and swung his belt but missed. CJ pushed Chester into the storage closet, flipped the rusty latch and closed the padlock. He snatched his hat off the floor and poked his head out the back door before trotting to the tow truck.

He slammed the heavy door closed and switched on the radio. The sheriff's department was converging on the landfill. No sign of the fugitives. Listening to the reports, he tore out of the back entrance, keeping his head low as he cruised through town. When he made it to the highway, he hauled ass for the old textile mill.

The dilapidated textile mill had been shut down due to high levels of asbestos. Locals avoided the place, except for the occasional group of teenagers ghost hunting or looking for a place to drink, and the out-of-state owners made no effort to revitalize the property. CJ discovered his writing shed during an inspection Commissioner Bristol had ordered as a part of his county cleanup efforts and as a failed attempt to light a fire under the mill owners. While CJ was escorting the inspectors through the woods to check the creek for contamination, he had spotted the old building. He'd read that many great writers had writing huts and he'd been on the lookout for his own. After the inspection, he returned to the shed and set up a desk and a chair there. He loved his hut and found the trickle of the creek relaxing. For months, the shed served him well as a place of solitude and creative meditation. Then it happened. An outsider invaded his private sanctuary. But with the invasion came an opportunity. He seized it, never caring about the identity of the perpetrator. Until now.

He stomped on the gas, pushing the tow truck to the limit. The roads were dead and the roadblocks gone. He was the only deputy not called to the landfill. He leaned forward as a vehicle approached in the oncoming lane. He whipped his head, rubbing his cowboy hat on the ceiling and knocking it off onto the steering wheel. He shifted his eyes to his rearview mirror and watched the news van fade into the distance. All the news outlets had been camped out on the Wisely property, reporting on the manhunt from that location. The sheriff's radio chatter sent them scurrying to the landfill. Those fools. He had the inside scoop on them. He pounded the steering wheel. And Peggy had the scoop on him.

He turned in front of the mill, drove down the side street to the rear of the facility and parked the truck in the back corner of the parking lot. Spinning on his heel, he assessed his surroundings before grabbing the grocery bag and his hat. He bumped the door closed with his hip and looked the truck up and down. If Peggy was right about new evidence, driving a tow truck with no trunk was gonna make this part of the clean up harder than usual.

He hustled down the familiar trail, twisting and turning through the underbrush. He stopped at the top of the elevated creek bank and looked down at the creek a few feet below. The water level was low, exposing large patches of sand and pebbles on the creek bed. "Uh, oh," he said, as he jumped down. The pebbles crunched under his feet as he walked towards the trickling water. He glanced over at his writing shed, teetering on the edge of the water.

Peggy nailed it. More evidence had appeared. As he squatted down to get a closer look, he heard the whining of an engine approaching. He hugged the bag to his chest and ran back and forth, looking for a place to hide. He jumped up to the trail and said, "Dang."

## Chapter Twenty

Willem stood on the footboards and scanned the area as he and Murven approached the textile mill. The facility was only a few miles from the landfill, but they'd followed the trails deep in the woods to keep away from the roads. He patted Murven's shoulder and pointed to the back end of the mill parking lot. Murven pulled the ATV to the edge of the woods and throttled down the engine.

Willem sat down, raised his visor and said, "That's Chester's truck."

Murven kicked the ATV into gear and drove up next to the tow truck. Willem slung his leg over the back end and jogged to the vehicle. He peeked in the window and looked back at Murven with a shrug. Backing away, he looked around the parking lot before running back. He pulled off his helmet and tossed it on the ground. "Trail," he said, heading towards the woods.

Murven hooked his helmet over the handle bars and followed. The trail narrowed as they trekked deeper into the woods. Willem tilted his head and listened to the sound of distant sirens whining through the trees. Energized by anxiety and agitation, his feet pounded the dirt below with a steady rhythm. Pushing a tree limb out of his face, he glanced back at Murven. "Nobody saw us, I reckon."

"Nope," Murven said. "Wonder if they'll find Handy?"

Willem shook his head and spit. No way anybody could find Handy in his natural habitat. The sound of running water grew louder and the sunlight grew brighter as the tops of the trees opened overhead. Willem spotted the top of CJ's writing shed, framed in the tree limbs, and he turned onto a smaller side trail. The creek came into view as Willem stepped out of the underbrush into the clearing at the top of the elevated creek bank. "Holy shit," he said, jumping down to the creek bed.

"Hot damn," Murven said, checking the trail behind him before leaping down the drop off. "Is he dead?"

Willem inched closer to the hobo lying on the ground, stopping with each step to look around. He nudged the body with his foot and leaned towards the man's face. "Yep."

Murven circled wide around Willem and the hobo, keeping his distance and stretching his neck to see the dead man's face. "What's all that shit in his beard?"

"Couldn't tell ya," Willem said, staring at the hobo. He drew in a deep breath and walked to the shed. The building sat crooked on the bank and leaned towards the creek, the back corner submerged in water. He gave the shed a push and waited for it to stop wobbling before pulling the door open.

Murven zipped past Willem and sprang inside, splashing the water under the shed. "Just a desk and a chair," he said, standing with his feet spread and rocking the building.

Willem turned, surveying the woods, then went back to inspect the hobo. He knelt down, holding his hands over the body without touching, not sure where to begin. From the corner of his eye, he saw Murven raising his hands. He jerked his head towards the trail and gasped.

"Well, well, well," CJ said from the top of the creek bank. "Looks like I caught y'all red handed."

"You set me up, you little shit," Willem said.

"Bullshit. I tried to help you two dumb shits. But that don't matter none now. Y'all are caught and I'm the hero." CJ pulled his radio off his belt. "Deddy, it's me."

"Keep off the radio, Junior!" the sheriff's voice blasted through the static.

"I caught 'em, Deddy! They killed another hobo!"

"Where are you?"

"At the creek behind the old textile mill."

"Keep 'em there. I'm headed your way."

CJ hung the radio back on his belt. "Y'all get down on your knees. Don't try nothing."

"What're you doing out here, anyway?" Murven said, hopping out of the shed and lowering himself to his knees.

"Don't you worry about it. Maybe I'll tell ya sometime when I'm interviewing your ass in prison."

"You're workin' with Wilbur." Willem stared at CJ and crossed his arms, making no effort to go down on his knees. "You're helping him frame me."

"Wilbur?" CJ bunched his lips and raised his eyebrows. "What makes you think that?"

"You're just playing games." Willem shook his head, eyeballing CJ. "You really don't give a shit."

CJ held the grocery bag with his hooked index finger and swung it by his leg, keeping the gun on Willem. He beamed for a moment, then broke the silence. "Why would I set you up? You two are dumb enough to get caught on your own. You tell me why you was killin' these hobos. Maybe I'll take it easy on you in my news story."

"Nobody's gonna read your shit," Murven said, sitting back on his feet.

"Murven, why don't you try runnin' or sumpin' so I can shoot ya."

"Why are you here?" Murven said, tossing a pebble in his hands.

"I tracked y'all from the landfill. Had a hunch you was gonna kill today."

"Stop talkin' to him, Murven. He's just lookin' for ways to twist shit." Willem spit and shifted his eyes to the left of CJ. He squinted to get a better look.

CJ rotated his head, following Willem's eyes. Before he could see anything, Peggy dropped out of a tree with her arm extended and clipped CJ's neck, taking him down with a flying clothesline. CJ fell to the creek bed, dropping his gun and the bag of files. His radio flew off his belt, smashed on a rock and went dead.

"Run, Willem!" Peggy shouted, her eyes glowing behind her camouflage face paint. "My plan ain't gonna work if y'all are here."

CJ groaned as he sat up on his side. Peggy jumped to the creek bed and charged, arm raised for an elbow drop. CJ twisted over onto both hands and kicked his right leg back, landing a mule kick on

Peggy's chest. Peggy's arms flung out to the side and she sailed backwards to the ground.

CJ lurched for his gun. Willem dove in front of him and snatched it up.

Peggy stood in front of CJ with her arms up and knees bent in attack position. CJ looked at Willem. "Shoot her!" he cried.

"I ain't shootin' nobody!" Willem said, moving out of the way as he watched Peggy hop on her toes and slap her own shoulders, prepping to whoop CJ's ass.

CJ turned back towards Peggy. "You're under arrest, hag!" He dropped his shoulder and ran towards her. Peggy ducked under his right arm, wrapping her right arm around his shoulder. She swung her left arm over CJ's left shoulder, grabbed his right wrist and slapped on a cobra clutch. She pulled him in tight and took him down with a leg sweep. As they smacked down on the sand and pebbles, CJ rolled out of the hold and crawled away backwards on his hands and knees, keeping his eyes on Peggy.

"You little shit! You ruined my plan!" Peggy shouted, springing to her feet and charging for CJ.

CJ stepped to the side and hip tossed Peggy to the ground. She rolled through the fall and scooped her arm between CJ's legs. In a burst of strength, she lifted CJ and body slammed him. She hopped on his back and slid her arms under his armpits, clasping her fingers behind his neck. She squeezed tight, locked in the full nelson, and whispered, "I'm gonna kill you," in CJ's ear.

CJ wiggled his hips and twitched his shoulders, unable to break free. "She's gonna kill me!" he shouted. "Shoot her, Willem!"

"Run, Willem!" Peggy wrapped her legs around CJ's waist. "Hurry!"

"Don't run! I can prove you're innocent! She'll kill me if y'all go!" CJ flapped his arms and feet.

"Run, Willem. I can prove you're innocent but y'all gotta go!" Peggy flexed her elbows out to the side and squeezed her knees, bending CJ's back and lifting his head off the ground.

Willem stood by the body, holding the gun by his leg. He looked over at Murven and said, "Dang."

# Chapter Twenty-One

Willem stood frozen. The sound of sirens rang in the distance, echoing through the woods. He squeezed the gun in his hand and looked down at the dead hobo. Rubbing his ear, he shifted his eyes to Peggy. He stretched his jaw from side to side as he watched her tighten her grip on her full nelson, causing CJ to squirm. Both CJ and Peggy knew something, yet he couldn't trust either one.

"Happy's on his way," Peggy hollered. "He'll be here any minute. Go!" Her teeth popped out of her mouth and she sucked them back in as she wrenched down on CJ's neck.

"Don't leave," CJ said, hoarse from the struggle. "She's gonna kill me."

"Let's git," Murven said, grabbing Willem's arm. "CJ's fulla shit."

"That's the smartest thang I ever heard Murven say." Peggy flexed her fingers. "I'll prove your innocence, hun. I promise."

Willem cocked his head to listen to the sirens. The sheriff and deputies were closing in fast. His jaw tightened as he watched Peggy forcing CJ's head closer to the water. He raised the gun, the grip slippery in his sweaty hand, but stopped himself before taking aim. Peggy and CJ were both bullshitters. They were impossible to believe. Even at gunpoint. As he relaxed his arm, he heard Murven breathing heavy and pacing behind him. Willem wiped his prints off the gun with his shirt and pointed up the creek with his thumb. As he dropped the gun in the creek, he turned to follow Murven, who had already headed upstream.

"Don't go! I need witnesses!" CJ hollered.

"Go to hell," Willem said over his shoulder.

CJ arched his back to keep his face out of the water as Peggy increased the pressure. "I framed you!" CJ's face touched the surface of the water. "But I didn't kill nobody! Peggy's gonna kill me!"

Willem stopped, stumbling forward from his own momentum. "What did you say!" he shouted.

"I found the bodies and took them to your shit pile." CJ spit water out of his mouth. "But I didn't kill 'em."

Willem lowered his head and pressed his arms down by his side. He walked with big strides to CJ and dropped down on his hand and knees to look CJ in the eye. "Why me?"

"You were the one with the shit pile." CJ tried to turn away.

"Who's the killer?" Willem asked, eye to eye with CJ.

"I don't know." CJ twisted his shoulders.

"Bullshit, you crybaby!" Peggy kneed CJ in the butt. "I followed you. I know you killed them hobos."

"The bodies just started showing up." CJ sniffed a drip of snot up his nose. "I saw an opportunity so I took it."

"Let him git up so I can whoop his ass," Willem said to Peggy.

"I'll do it for you, sugar." Peggy shifted her weight on CJ's back. "You better run."

Willem sat back on his knees and turned his good ear towards the mill to listen. He saw Murven standing on the creek bed below the trail.

"They're close," Murven said, looking back and forth between the trail and Willem.

Willem looked at CJ. He held his palm up to Murven and shook his head. "Find that bag CJ had with him."

Murven waved back and jumped up to the trail.

"Haul ass, sugar!" Peggy said through her gritted teeth.

"Not yet. I need proof he framed me." Willem kept his eye on Murven, who was digging through the underbrush.

"I can prove it. Now git!"

The sirens wailed louder. Willem checked upstream and downstream, then he looked back up to the trail. He lost sight of Murven. As he stood up, he squinted his eyes and said, "How did you know, Peggy?"

"My sources told me."

"She ain't got no sources," CJ said. "She's got bugs everywhere to listen to people."

"I can prove this little shit is the killer," Peggy said, out of breath. Her fingers slipped but she managed to keep her grip. "I got video of CJ and the dead hobo."

"Murven!" Willem hollered.

"Over here," Murven said, holding the plastic bag in the air. "Wait. There's more shit."

Willem looked down at Peggy. He needed all the proof he could get to clear their names. "Where's the video?"

Peggy ignored him, straining to sink CJ's face in the water.

"Found it!" Murven shouted from the woods. He

stood in the underbrush along the trail, raising Peggy's bag over his head. The oversized purse clanked as he lifted his knees high to walk clear of the bushes. Once on the trail, he opened the purse and reached his hand inside.

"Stay outta that, you dumbass. Give it to me." Peggy jerked her head towards Murven, losing control of CJ. Her fingers split apart and she lifted her chest off CJ. Grinding her teeth, she squeezed CJ's arms behind his back into a double chicken wing.

Murven pulled out the camera and shook it off. He hooked the strap on his shoulder and sniffed in the bag.

"Stay outta there, jackass!"

"Damn, Peggy," Murven said. "You having a picnic out here?" He tossed the grease-soaked paper plate with the smudges of mashed potatoes and gravy down to the creek bed.

Willem looked at the plate and then at the hobo. "Mashed potatoes," he said, as he bent over the hobo.

"Smells like it," Murven said, sniffing inside the bag.

"That's mashed potatoes in the hobo's beard." Willem turned to look at Peggy. "Peggy? You feed the hobo?"

"Holy shit! Holy Shit!" CJ hollered. "I told ya!"

"What?" Murven said, pointing the camera down at Peggy and CJ.

Peggy tucked her head and grunted. She lifted CJ and slammed him into the ground. "You little shit! You ruined everything!" She jumped in the creek and snatched the gun out of the water. "I'm sorry, Willem. It was supposed to be CJ. I never meant for you to git caught up in this mess. He kept moving the damn bodies!"

CJ raised himself to his hands and knees. "You crazy witch! You set me up!"

"Shut up!" Peggy fired a shot in the ground in front of CJ. "You ruined my story!"

CJ lunged back and rolled behind Willem.

"Move, Willem!" Peggy shouted.

"Don't let her kill me!" CJ hugged Willem's ankles and ducked his head. "I'll confess to everything!"

Willem looked down at CJ, who was trembling at his feet. They had known each other their entire lives. CJ had always been a whiney, conniving brat, sheltered by his daddy. As Willem bent over to pry CJ's hands loose, he looked into his teary eyes. The fear was real. As much as he hated CJ, he believed him. CJ was opportunistic, warped enough to move a dead body for his own gain, but too much of a coward to actually kill anybody.

Willem broke CJ's grip and jumped to the side. "How could you kill all those men?" he said to Peggy, stepping out of CJ's reach.

Peggy sucked her teeth, adjusted her grip on the gun and then fired a shot into the ground between Willem and CJ.

"Dammit, Peggy!" Willem dashed into the woods.

"Help me, Willem!" CJ cried. "I'm sorry I framed you!" He scooted backwards across the creek bed, looking for a place to take cover. He looked at Murven, who was videotaping, and hollered into the camera, "It was me! I framed Willem for the murders! I found the bodies and put 'em in his shit pile! I framed him for the fire, too! I don't wanna die!"

"The fire?" Peggy said, holding the gun with both hands. "You are a little turd." She aimed at CJ's head and walked out of the water.

"Freeze," Sheriff Happy shouted from the trail. "Drop your weapon."

Peggy looked up stream at a deputy with his gun aimed at her. She looked downstream at another deputy who also had her in his sights. She tossed her gun on the ground and put her hands up in the air. Her lips curled into an evil grin as she adjusted her teeth. With a wink, she spun around and took off into the woods.

Sheriff Happy leapt from the trail and sprinted

across the creek. He hooked Peggy with his right arm and carried her back, kicking and screaming.

"Lock her up," the sheriff said, handing Peggy over to the two deputies.

"You ruined everything, you little shit!" Peggy shouted, as the deputies carried her down the trail.

"Wait!" Willem hollered, pacing in the creek, keeping his distance from the sheriff. "What about Wilbur? Peggy!" He listened but her shouting faded away.

CJ stood up and wiped the tears from his eyes. "I caught 'em red handed, Deddy."

"Sheriff," Murven said, waving the camera in the air. "You're gonna wanna see this."

"Don't need to. I heard him hollerin' from the road." Sheriff Happy kicked CJ in the butt. "Git your ass to the car."

Willem stood in the creek, arms bent, ready to take off into the woods. He watched Murven, who was videoing the deputies as they surrounded him. One deputy took the camera. Another held Murven by the arm. Willem locked eyes with the sheriff and said, "I didn't kill nobody."

"I'm starting to believe that," the sheriff said, "but running ain't helping you any. Just come in so we can focus on the investigation and figure this shit out."

Willem nodded as he relaxed his shoulders. "By the way," he said, "Jesper Holliday wants to kill me."

"I'll see what I can do." The sheriff put his hand on Willem's neck and walked him to the trail.

Willem jumped up and headed towards the mill. He'd gotten caught in the middle of the publicity war between CJ and Peggy but survived the battle. He had what he needed to clear his name. With CJ's fire confession, he could start rebuilding his reputation in the county. And for the first time since his parents had died, reconciliation with his brothers seemed possible. He had to find Wilbur. But that would have to wait for another day.

"You call the news yet?" he heard Murven say to the sheriff.

Willem smiled a half smile, spit and said, "Dang."

## Epilogue

Willem slipped in a dip and lay back on the couch, resting his head on Cindy's leg. He held up the local section of the newspaper and read the front page. "Willem Wisely and Murven Holliday Cleared of All Charges," the headline read. On the bottom left under the fold, a smaller headline read "Wisely Arsonist Still at Large."

"You think they'll ever find out who started the fire?" Cindy asked.

Willem shrugged and shifted his eyes to the bottom right, where a picture of Murven giving a thumbs up jumped off the page. The murder investigation had created the media circus that both Peggy and CJ had hoped it would. The story received a brief mention in the national news, but neither of them received any acclaim. Murven emerged as the break-out celebrity. He appeared on the news and executed the lines he'd rehearsed to perfection while on the run. After seeing himself on screen, he decided his calling was to be a reporter. Taking a cue from Peggy, he started his own news channel on YouTube.

Willem smiled a half smile and spread his arms to open the paper. Photos of Peggy on the witness stand covered all of the second page. The investigation revealed a mountain of evidence against her. The medical reports concluded that the hobos died from poisoning, and Peggy's special seasoning was a perfect match in the chemical analysis. That, in addition to all the evidence uncovered in her trailer and the hours of video she had of the dead hobos, gave Peggy little choice but to accept a plea bargain. With her misguided knack for publicity, she negotiated a plea bargain that allowed her to outline her scheme on the witness stand in a courtroom open to the media. She explained to the court and the cameras—incriminating herself without regard—how she improvised and adapted each time that dumbass CJ derailed her plans. She boasted about how she manipulated Willem and Murven to make the story more exciting, but remained cryptic about how she obtained the photos of Wilbur. The media speculated that she stumbled upon Wilbur by chance and took his picture covertly while scoping out the hobo jungle. Peggy neither confirmed nor denied those reports, citing the fifth commandment as her defense. After three days of dramatic testimony, she received life in prison.

Willem squeezed the dip in his lip and turned the page. CJ's official headshot was tucked in next to an ad for Mars Diner. Peggy's trial had eclipsed CJ's efforts to leverage his own case. He went through three lawyers before finding one who would argue his plea of guilty by reason of possession. He insisted he was possessed by a demon that forced him to frame people so none of it was his fault. He claimed that confessing exorcised the demon, causing him to forget all of his tidbits. The jury found him guilty by reason of insanity. He was sentenced to treatment at the state psychiatric hospital, where he began writing his semi-autobiographical account of demonic possession in the form of a paranormal romance novel.

Willem chucked the local section of the newspaper on the floor and shook out the political page. He clicked his tongue and showed Cindy the picture of Terry Bristol and Poot Barber shaking hands. Terry managed to take credit for the success of the investigation. After the trials ended, he reported the success of his county clean-up plan and officially announced his run for governor. After some back-room dealing, Poot emerged as his biggest supporter for the governor's race and hinted at the possibility of running for chief county commissioner once Terry was elected governor.

"You talk to Willard?" Cindy asked.

"Yep." Willem laid the newspaper on his chest. "I'm meeting him, Walmer and Wilton out at the barn next week. We're gonna decide what to do with the property."

"Any news about Wilbur?"

"Nah, he's still missing."

"Willem! Cindy!" Murven's voice startled them both.

"What the hell," Willem said, as Murven burst through the door.

"Turn on the news," Murven said. "Peggy escaped."

Willem sat up, spit in his drink bottle and said, "Dang."

## Rob Smith Books

Thank you for reading! I'm Rob Smith and I write under the names R.D. Smith, Lick Darsey and Rob Douglas.

Please visit my website to see more of my books and to learn about more opportunities to keep up with me and my projects.

robsmithbooks.com

## About the Author

R.D. Smith is a North Carolina native who spent his formative years developing a keen eye for all things redneck. He earned his BA in Psychology from UNC-Chapel Hill then "worked for a few years." In 2001, R.D. sold everything he owned and moved to Christchurch, New Zealand where he earned his MA in Theatre and Film Studies from the University of Canterbury. He went on to live and work in China and Japan. He recently moved home after 14 years abroad and has managed to maintain his redneck sensibilities through it all.